The
Question Authority

The

Question Authority

a novel

Rachel Cline

 Red Hen Press | *Pasadena, CA*

Book layout by Mark E. Cull

Library of Congress Cataloging-in-Publication Data

Names: Cline, Rachel, 1957– author.
Title: The Question Authority : a novel / Rachel Cline.
Description: First edition. | Pasadena, CA : Red Hen Press, [2019]
Identifiers: LCCN 2018055869| ISBN 9781597098984 (pbk.) | ISBN
1597098981 (pbk.)
Classification: LCC PS3603.L555 Q47 2019 | DDC 813/.6—dc23
LC record available at https://lccn.loc.gov/2018055869

Publication of this book has been made possible in part through the
financial support of Ann Beman.

The National Endowment for the Arts, the Los Angeles County Arts
Commission, the Dwight Stuart Youth Fund, the Max Factor Family
Foundation, the Pasadena Tournament of Roses Foundation, the Pasadena Arts & Culture Commission and the City of Pasadena Cultural Affairs Division, the City of Los Angeles Department of Cultural
Affairs, the Audrey & Sydney Irmas Charitable Foundation, the Ah-
manson Foundation, the Meta & George Rosenberg Foundation, the
Kinder Morgan Foundation, the Allergan Foundation, and the Rior-
dan Foundation all partially support Red Hen Press.

First Edition
Published by Red Hen Press
www.redhen.org

"Good morning little school girl, can I go home with you?"

—traditional

Wednesday
February 18, 2009

1

Nora

BROOKLYN, NEW YORK

Sometimes I get grief and resentment confused. Also fear and anticipation. It's not that I don't know what the words mean, but that whatever it seems like I should be feeling (grief over my mother's death, excitement about a potential date) is not what I am feeling. It's been like this since I was a kid, but it's taken me until recently to put it together: I have a fundamental emotional wiring problem. Is fifty-three too old to be learning new things about your psyche?

The trouble of the moment—what's keeping me awake on a work night—is the problem of my lost cat. "Lost" is a misnomer; I let him out. I had this idea that by letting him roam I was honoring his essential cat-ness, his life as a hunter and wanderer. Only it's February and I live in New York City and, even though Brooklyn Heights is a tree-lined neighborhood where you rarely see a car traveling at more than parking-seeking speed, it's been almost three days now. People have found him before, and called me—he has a tag—but that was only one night away, at most.

Given the timing, it's likely that my cat-freedom gambit was some kind of hedge against my mother's death. Adeline died eighteen months ago: three months before I adopted the cat. Prior to her death, I'd convinced myself that she wasn't all

9

that important to me—that her role in my life was more like that of an eccentric aunt than the woman who'd breastfed me till I was three (or so she claimed). Every single time she saw me, she opened with a criticism ("You look pale." "What happened to your hair?" "*What* are you wearing?"); she'd never noticed or admitted that I was fundamentally depressed from age thirteen to thirty-five (when: Prozac); and—adding insult to injury—she did none of what they call "advance planning" for her own demise. She left me not only broke but awash in legal and financial perplexities. I had no choice but to move back into this apartment, the apartment I grew up in, after I'd sold its contents. Maybe by letting the cat roam, I felt better about feeling trapped myself?

In any case, I was proud of my liberated cat, of trusting him to find his own way home—it mirrored the way I was raised. Back then, I was not the only kid around here with an apartment key on the same length of twine as the key to her roller skates. I had a best friend, and a three-dollar-a-week allowance, and—as long as we stayed on the right side of Atlantic Avenue and were home for dinner—we did what we pleased. Beth did, anyway. She was the brave one. But that's another story.

Tin Man, please come home.

Thursday
February 19, 2009

2

Nora

I wake up on Thursday morning expecting the cat to be with me, emanating warmth and profound disinterest from his customary sleeping spot in the V between my butt and my feet. The light in the bedroom is gray and bright—unmistakably after seven—but finding that Tin Man's spot is empty throws my whole morning routine into question. I hate my job, I hate my life, I live in the emptiest apartment in the universe . . . what's the point? Under normal circumstances, I would just bury my face in the cat and tell him how much I love him and how little I want to get up, but with no cat, I'm stymied. I don't want to say that stuff out loud to *myself*—it sounds pathetic and ridiculous. I sit up and gaze dolefully at the stupendous view. The harbor is silver-gray and choppy and the orange lozenge of the Staten Island Ferry chugging by is perfect in color, shape, and size. The cranes and gantries of Port Newark have a poetic quality in the hazy distance. Even Governor's Island looks charming. What am I to do with my conflicting emotions?

I live in my grandfather's apartment. He's long dead, and it's got nothing in it but the crap I bought at IKEA when I moved in, but it's a penthouse with four bedrooms, three baths, a library, a music room, and two working fireplaces—a relic from a time when a poet could actually get rich. Back then, brownstones were going up everywhere (like condos, these days) and were far too *hoi polloi* for a grand figure like my poet granddad. Now, it's worth a fortune—even after the recent crash. But I am not allowed to sell it under the terms of his trust. This is something my mother might have fixed before she died, if she'd been willing to admit that dying was in the cards, but she wasn't, and didn't, and so. Here I am again in Brooklyn Heights.

To anyone who didn't grow up here, the first impression is always of wealth. Walking under old, leafy trees, you catch glimpses of chic sitting rooms and private gardens; historic landmarks and secret-seeming alleys; adorable carriage houses and ornate mansions; as well as churches for all comers. Standing at the edge of the Promenade to watch the sunset, you will invariably hear someone (perhaps your own inner real estate agent) pronounce the words "million-dollar view."

When my grandfather got here, in the early twenties, it was "America's first suburb," and indeed a wealthy enclave. But when my mother dragged me back to this apartment in 1963, the Heights was actually a fairly Bohemian place. That first summer, I attended a settlement house day camp with black and Puerto Rican kids where we sang spirituals and spent our days in city parks and pools. The formerly grand hotels that dotted the neighborhood were all then sheltering welfare recipients, but the ethnic mix of kids at camp came from nearby apartments—as did artists and writers and folk singers and even, briefly, Marilyn Monroe.

And now, in 2009, it's changing again. Lots of empty storefronts, but no more welfare hotels. On the street I still see people I recognize from the old days: the grumpy shoemaker;

Julie Something's little sister, now model-beautiful and married to a famous artist; the homeless woman with wild hair, who I fear may be Josh Pinsky's mother. The Key Food is still a tragedy, but there is now also a Gristedes and something called Garden of Eden, where you can, most of the time, buy a decent-looking artichoke. There are long waiting lists for Friends, Saint Ann's, and Packer, but they say P.S. 8 has a new principal and is turning around.

I do eventually get out of bed, shower, dress, and set out for work. Yes, another thing I can't complain about to anyone, ever: I walk to work. It takes about fifteen minutes, but today it takes twenty, because I am scanning every gated gap between buildings, every shrubbery, delivery entrance, impassible/filthy patch of former snow, and tempting garbage pile for some sign of my missing companion. And so, I am late. By the time I have clocked in, dumped my coat in my cubicle, and logged into my email, I find I have been summoned to my boss's office for a meeting that began five minutes earlier. This is not a common occurrence.

Jocelyn waves me in and starts talking before I have even sat down. I am distracted by her breakfast. In her chapped left hand she holds a cup of diet vanilla yogurt. With her right she pours in half a package of M&M's and then begins to stir with a plastic spoon. The colored dyes from the candy swirl into the white gel, making it look like a bath product or a toilet cleaner. I'm so appalled that I don't really hear what she's saying until my brain reacts to the word "pedo-whatever," in close proximity to the word "McGillicuddy," which is Jocelyn's universal nickname for all public school teachers. She concludes with the statement, "So I'm looking for a quick turn from you, Nora. There's a hearing on for Monday morning," and she pushes an accordion file at me. I reach forward instinctively because the accordion file is unevenly loaded and balanced on top of all the other things that live on Jocelyn's desk, including numerous coffee-cart napkins, a calendar from the Brooklyn Botanic Garden that's still showing last year's cherry blossoms, and what I can only assume are several years' worth of memoranda from HR. She said, "Monday morning," but as it's now almost ten on Thursday, what I really have is about twelve hours. And did I hear that right? Are we settling a case with a child molester?

"I've never settled a personnel case before," I blurt.

"Yeah, it's the same thing as liability or special ed. Just look at the comps, come up with an offer, and then back off like twenty percent."

"But the guy's a pervert and we're settling?"

"Yeah. He got caught before, too." She pats the file folder. "Don't get too mashed into the details; just offer."

She's acting like this is business as usual but it's not, it can't be. I've only been here three months but . . . "Can't we just fire him?"

"First off, they have a union, right? They have due process—documentation, a warning, probable cause, blah-de-blah-blah." She shakes the fountain of red hair off her shoulders. Jocelyn has the head of a twelve-year-old girl on the body of a fifty-five-year-old Irish broad. Sometimes I think she's like my alternate-reality self, the one who grew up in a row house in Queens instead of a palatial co-op in Brooklyn Heights, and who was never a freelancer or a Talking Heads fan but stuck it out for forty years of paper pushing at the Education Department, and who never doubted that course. I guess I'm supposed to be nodding at her explanation but it still doesn't make any sense to me.

"I thought we had 'zero tolerance.'"

"Think about it. They're not that easy to catch in the act—I mean, that's happened, but like *then* someone calls the cops."

I try to picture how a pedophile operates in a school. Of course, I already know: he writes understanding notes in the margins of the girl's homework, tells her she's pretty, that she can come to him any time she ever "needs to talk."

"The girl's a teenager," Jocelyn explains, "so half the time they think they're in love. It's like a spy movie, you know?"

In eighth grade, my best friend was fucking our teacher— as were several others at our fancy girls' school, the Academy. In 1971, the word "pedophile" was not so commonplace and Bob Rasmussen was all of twenty-six, not what we then called a "dirty old man." But I have come around to the realization, and it's taken me a long time to get there, that he was a predator. "So, what do we offer in a case like this?"

The cases I've had to settle so far (which is what I do, settle lawsuits—think insurance adjuster) have been mundane: staff members claiming they were wrongfully terminated or made to work "out of category"—the worst-case scenario is that we wind up paying them what they want, or giving them their jobs back. It's depressing, but no one is materially harmed. (Well, except maybe the schoolchildren whose schools don't have science books or working toilets because of all the money the department has to spend on lawsuits.) Anyway, when we settle we just give the other side some grand sum and, in return, they stipulate that they won't sue us anymore, or defame us, or join a class action. I can't imagine what the agreement could possibly say in a case like this one: we'll pay you to go away and in return you'll pretend you weren't really a pedophile?

"What we offer is that he walks away from the job for something less than what it would cost to keep him on payroll till he retires. If he won't take that, we keep paying him but he spends the rest of his working life in the rubber room."

"There's no version where he gets punished?"

"The rubber room is a lot like jail, if you ask me."

"Except you go home at three o'clock and get the summer off!" This is pissing me off more than I would have expected. I'm somewhat inured to the whole sexual predator thing at this point—it doesn't shock me, it just makes me sad—but I have a lot of resentment about how much people get paid, compared to my paltry $48K. I never minded being broke when I thought I'd be unbroke as soon as my mother died. Now I see how everyone else my age has this figured out by now—even fucking perverts. "I might need some help, Jocelyn. Can one of the attorneys consult?"

"I don't have an attorney to spare right now and anyway it was that nitwit Jodie Koo that let this one sit around for two and a half months without realizing there was a hearing scheduled. I'm giving it to you because you're fast. Don't even read the file. Just hold your nose and settle."

Jodie got the boot about a week ago, I think. There's this illusion that city jobs are safe, but that's only if you're in a permanent civil service title. People get fired all the time around here. So I pick up the accordion file, wrap my arms around it to contain the loose papers jammed inside, and nod my "Yes, boss." Jocelyn's door is propped open by a plaster bust of Elvis Presley, which is highly unlikely to be hers.

3
Bob

From: bear@nyc.rr.com
To: PBJ@nyc.rr.com
Date sent: Feb 18 2009 12:32 AM
Subject: On the Road

Peanut,

Here I am in Tuba City, at what they call a "family restaurant." I thought you would appreciate the irony, as I make my journey of fatherly remorse. The wait-a-little is cute. Just now, she caught me staring and, to my absolute amazement, smiled—probably why I decided it was time to make my report to you. I guess, out here, even a used-up hulk like me might still look like a ticket out. I'm wearing Dad's old Rolex, which is definitely a rich guy's watch, so maybe it's that. You convinced me it was too beautiful to leave in the lockbox. When was that? Five years ago? He'd been dead for ten. You said no one was ever going to mistake me for a Connecticut Yankee insurance man and that was true. But in Tuba City I could be anyone!

"Where you headed?" she asks me. She refills my water glass and I see she bites her nails like I do. Involuntarily, I close my fingers into my fist so she won't see the connection.

"Laramie," I say. "Flew into Phoenix though, so I could drive through here, again. It's been maybe thirty years."

She nods, but without interest. It's hard to imagine someone finding this landscape boring but I guess if you're seventeen and it's where you live . . . She's barely seventeen. And she has that mix of cockiness and uncertainty that always kills me. I decide I'll call her "Catnip." Don't worry, I'm still on the straight and narrow, here. But part of that is telling the truth about it from the get-go, so there's no tantalizing forbidden thing, just ordinary desire that happens to everyone. Right?

"So, what's in Laramie?"

If I were on the make I'd tell her about Doria. No one suspects a dad. But I lie: "Just on a break."

"I've never been on a vacation," says Catnip, without self-pity. "If I had the time off, I don't think I'd spend it driving around stupid towns like this one, though, but to each his own."

"I'll drink to that," I say, lifting my water glass. But there it ends, so I'm going to put the laptop away and get back in the Chevy Cruze, which is surprisingly fun to drive.

Pulled over:

This landscape looked so different when I had you with me. Grown-up you, I mean—the trip I think of as our honeymoon. We were listening to *Moby-Dick* on tape. You'd never read it. "All talk, no whale," you said, and I was shocked at your ignorance. I gave you a "teacher" look, and you called me "Miss Crabtree" and we thought that was the funniest thing ever because we were so happy, then. Happy Version 2.

Happy Version 1 is ancient history, of course: holding Doria's sweaty little hand when it fit into mine like a baby mouse. Sleeping together, all of us in a pile, when the kids still called me Daddy and thought I could do no wrong. Watching Archer learn how to flirt by hanging around with girls twice his age. Chasing your own sweet self through the mirror maze at the Topsy Turvy House.

But let's go back to Version 2: your bare feet on the dashboard, that stupid toe ring you bought at Wall Drug. Lounging by the pool in the middle of the night. I made up new constellations and tried to fool you, Brooklyn girl. The Dragon's Tooth, the Great Loom, the Salt Crystals. You said, "I could see that." You said they should be called "Cold Fire" and "Light Storm," like fast cars. Your accent made it sound tough instead of sappy. Or was I just too far gone? I'm going to look for that motel we stayed in, near Flagstaff. The morning we left, there were girls in the pool. I heard them but I didn't look. I thought I was cured—that finding you again after twenty-odd years had cured me.

I didn't bring the fifteen cassettes of *Moby-Dick* with me this trip. I've got Jeremy Irons reading *Lolita*. He sounds like he wrote the thing, or lived it. But no one will ever pity Humbert, not even me.

I was smart to give myself a good running start—plenty of highway for me to go all Woody Guthrie on, plenty of versions of small-town America to remind me of where I didn't wind up: waves of grain, ribbons of highway, Tucson to Tucumcari, don't forget Winona . . . I was so caught up in those images, that fantasy of escape. This is how I know I've changed: Nabokov's version is my version now, where bits of roadside refuse pose as flowers and the placidity of cows is a plea to be made into meat. I used to think I might write a novel someday, or at least a song. Nope. What I produced, all I produced are Archer and Doria and Naomi's ghost.

In a life overpopulated with uncalculated risks, gross oversights, and shithead moves, my kids' pretentious names turned out to be whoppers. Archer was supposed to be a doer, a warrior in the world. I don't have to connect the dots of that irony for you. And Doria was meant to be seaworthy, golden—only instead of Naomi's beauty and my ego, she got the reverse and now she's a ghost ship, sunk in the Great Plains somewhere, pretending to be an orphan. She never got over the loss of her mother, and I'm worthless since I didn't show up at her wedding. I didn't think she really wanted me there, but that's a ratshit excuse, and I could have at least made an effort. I did send them that tandem bicycle—I thought that was kind of brilliant for a couple with one blind member, who live in a flat place, and one of whom could definitely use a little exercise. But I didn't say any of that. I just wrote "Have fun, I love you." Hell, what do you say to your thirty-five-year-old daughter who hates you on the occasion of her second marriage? What am I going to say to her tomorrow, more to the point? "I'm sorry," is so old, and so out of character. I'll say it, of course, but she's not going to accept it. I'd turn around right now if I didn't think *you'd* never speak to me again. It's just that whenever I play the scene out in my head it goes south after about the third sentence—after *I'm sorry* but before *I love you more than anything in the world.* She won't believe me; why should she?

There's a remedy for this line of thought—a fantasy that starts with that nail-bitten hand, which I casually cover with mine on the yellow Formica counter, and then look up to see the look on her face, if there's a flicker. There is. I look away, out the window, and ask Catnip about herself. *If you could live anywhere in the world, where would it be?* She smiles a little, but resists, says something sarcastic. Oh, a feisty one. I always like the feisty ones.

I pulled over and called you—left a coded message: "Road trouble." Then I tried Henry—that's what sponsors are for, isn't it? He picked up but, like you, he's at work. He said I should work on my inventory while I'm driving. He said I'm still in denial, that I haven't gone far enough. I still say that until I got caught I was just a horny young guy like any other. The remorse, regret, obsess, seduce, self-hate go-round didn't kick in till I was in that holding cell in Window Rock, till Dad showed up. I've been meaning to ask you how much of all that you remember. We never talk about what happened that night, or after that, to you girls. Am I still allowed to give you a writing assignment?

I just called Doria, thought I'd give her a heads-up, let myself off the hook a little, right? It didn't go so well:

"Tonight's not good, Dad."

"Well, I didn't mean tonight, obviously. I've got plans for tonight—" I don't know why I lie about shit like that when it's perfectly obvious I'm just covering up.

"Tomorrow, after church, might work," she said. "First Baptist. Anyone in town can tell you how to get there."

I was about to ask what time that is but she hung up. I guess anyone can also tell me when "after church" is, too. At least she said "after"; I don't think I could have managed "at" or "in." And maybe that means they'll invite me over for donuts or whatever. My parents used to take us out for ice cream. But they were Episcopalians.

Later:

Checked into the Motel 6 in Shiprock to watch girl-porn on my laptop like the disgusting old pervert my daughter believes me to be. I tell myself it will be easier to own up to my crimes tomorrow if I can gin up enough self-disgust tonight. But it's always the same old problem—how much is enough? Long day, Peanut. Time to hit send.

4

Naomi Rasmussen

(B. MARCH 1950, D. SEPTEMBER 1982)

When I went by the Academy that first day in 1968, that was the first time I really saw how unlike the rest of them we were. I'd been just a kid myself, really, when we got to Brooklyn—when Bob was teaching at that public school where all the kids were black. Those people felt more like *my people* even though they were nothing like it. But waiting for him at the Academy, I saw how we looked to the mothers there—that we were from the wrong part of town, even though we lived around the corner. The Academy mommies wore their sunglasses on top of their heads like they had a second set of eyes up there, and they had no socks on with their tennis shoes. Back home, not wearing socks was like not wearing a bra—a sure sign that you come from filth and it won't be long before you're back to it. In first grade, I had no socks and I won't ever forget that feeling.

The Academy building was just as hard to figure—a mansion, surely, but stuck between its neighbors shoulder to shoulder just like our brokedown brownstone around the corner, like all the houses in Brooklyn, it seemed like. And then there came Bob Rasmussen, such a show-off, with his cowboy boots and his blanket vest and his wavy red hair. . . . *That's my husband*, I thought, and I was proud to stand there with Archer on my hip. We looked like freaks.

We didn't yet say that word to mean "hippies," but still I was happy that we were different, and young, and free.

Being dead gives a person a lot of leeway. No joy, but perspective. You girls may judge us now, but Bob depended on me and that made my life make sense. I was the keeper of keys and buyer of food; I paid the bills, kept gas in the camper van, did the cleaning, bookkeeping, writing out of mimeos, and filing of negatives. I kept track of your nicknames. I braided your hair. It was a role I knew how to play—watched my ma do it. I knew she wasn't happy, but I saw how it was right for her anyway. Happy isn't everything. And for a long time I didn't even know what I'd got, that our life wasn't just like every other life a girl might marry into, when all she cares about is getting away from where she was.

5

Nora

On the way back to my cubicle from Jocelyn's office I pass the backs of three of my coworkers—we are referred to as "paralegals" but are in fact "Special Clerical Associates (provisional)" in the eyes of the civil service, and thus paid like secretaries. The desks of my fellow Bartlebys are all half-buried in file folders. Their monitor screens are plastered with spreadsheets; their gray-beige cube walls peppered with evidence of girlfriends, boyfriends, children, vacations . . . I've been here for three months and have not decorated mine at all. What would I post, pictures of Tin Man? I'm sure no one around here wonders about my personal life, anyway. I suspect most of them don't even know my name.

I put the accordion file down next to my monitor, take my seat, and rattle my mouse. I realize I'm really upset. I am not usually very concerned with politics, or justice, or things like that (which I think is what makes me reasonably good at this job—or at any rate fast, as Jocelyn has observed) but this case is different. I assume the guy is guilty—I don't have to read a word to make that leap. Sure, there could be a crazy girl making false accusations, or a jilted lover with a vendetta, or even a misinterpretation of clumsy but not criminal behavior, but these things are not nearly as likely as a middle-aged man thinking it might be fun to seduce a teenaged girl, which is probably a crime even older than prostitution, except that I don't think we even started calling it a crime until . . . sometime after World War II? Am I wrong about that?

A couple months ago I got an email from Trina Franklin, one of my former classmates at the Academy—the rare African American one. She said some of them were hiring a lawyer over what happened to us in eighth grade and did I want to join. They think they might get Gloria Allred. I said no, because I couldn't picture complaining about the minor shit that Rasmussen did with me, but it made me wonder again about Beth. Did she ever look back on that experience as an episode of abuse rather than hot sex and wild adventure (as it seemed to her at thirteen)? But even in the Internet Age, a person named Beth Alice Cohen is hard to find, especially if you're not sure what state she's living in. And a person named Nora Falsington Buchbinder is a slam dunk, which means she's never looked for me. In fact, she could dial my old ULster 5 phone number from back then and get my mother's answering machine, even now. I haven't had the heart to throw it away.

6

Nora

Eighth grade: I'm staring out the window at the leaves on the tree outside. They are light green outlined in brown with just a tiny orange line between. The green is too bright and the orange next to it clashes. They look like the colors in one of those psychedelic posters from The Fillmore. Rasmussen is reading to us from *Lady Sings the Blues*, Billie Holiday's autobiography. He's always reading to us about black people. Being read aloud to is a big part of our curriculum here, which seems like cheating to me but I am perfectly happy to sit here looking at the tree and picturing the Baltimore row houses where Billie scrubbed people's stoops for a nickel each, with her own brush and can of Bon Ami. Since I grew up in the city, I can always picture the lives of the people we read about. I know what a city street looks like, and what a pimp is, and now I know that the group of men drinking out of brown paper bags near the bus stop is "the corner wine club," that the guys in white robes on the subway are disciples of the prophet Elijah Muhammad. What I can't picture are the country clubs and pep squads in the books I get from the Scholastic book club, or what Nancy Drew's "powder-blue roadster" looks like. Where do kids play in places where there are no vacant lots, or fire stairs, or construction sites—where the roofs are not flat enough to run around on?

I've bragged about Bob Rasmussen to my neighborhood friends—he's incredibly cool and weird at the same time. He's twenty-six, has a beard and wears cowboy boots and rides a motorcycle named "Babe the Blue Ox." Kids hang around at his house after school and he lets us listen to his records and read his magazines and Naomi, his wife, sometimes does projects with little Doria and Archer that we can do, too. Like tie-dyeing. I don't like little kids so I avoid that part. In fact, I avoid the whole Bob's-house-as-hangout thing, but I brag about it anyway.

I'm watching Beth, who sits across the U of desks from me—he doesn't let us sit together anymore because we giggle too much. She is drawing in her notebook, or writing. She's the worst speller I've ever seen. Sometimes I think she's a lot stupider than I am but not because of how she is as a friend; just some of the things she's interested in—like fashion designers—are stupid and she doesn't really like to read. She's also boy-crazy. She would never try to describe the leaves out the window. She doesn't come from an artistic family. When I showed her the star charts painted on the ceiling in my grandfather's library, she asked why you would put something so fancy in a place where no one would really see it.

I am going to write a poem about that tree outside, and it's also going to be about The Fillmore Auditorium and Billie Holiday singing in a whorehouse, and this crazy private school with only white girls in it reading her biography when there are race riots going on like a mile away. That's why there are so many girls here from other neighborhoods—the public schools they were supposed to go to are too scary now.

"Okay," Bob says, getting up from his reading posture and stretching his arms over his head so that his T-shirt goes up and shows the arrow of orange hair on his belly, which I can't help but look at even though it's totally repulsive. "It's time for Rasmatazz." While we are getting out our pencils and opening our notebooks, Beth asks, "Didn't we just do one of these?"

"You mean just last week? Yeah. We did. We're going to keep doing it until you get it right." He's smirking when he says this, of course, and everyone laughs. "Anyone remember what we're up to?"

"Ninety seconds!" Trina Franklin announces, in a tone that sounds like, "It's my birthday!" I knew the answer to that question, too, but would have gone through Chinese finger-nail torture before letting him know I am interested in his experiment. I hated it at fifteen seconds and was in a rage at thirty.

When he says "Go," everyone else starts writing immediately—already conditioned like sheep. If we have nothing to say, we are supposed to just write our names over and over but I have never stooped to that. I'm not worried about having nothing to say, but his assumption that he has the right to read anything that happens to be going through my head at this moment really bothers me so I spend the first ten seconds or so coming up with something that I feel is Rasmussen-proof. The first time, all I wrote was "The End," which I thought was pretty good. This time, I'm going to go with the tree outside— no emotions or opinions, just straight description:

The leaves on the tree outside are ugly. Orange and green at the same time like the colors of a pop art poster. How does nature

come up with this stuff? I hate the way people say "Mother Na-
ture," and picture a little old lady in a bonnet like Old Mother
Hubbard. Nature is not a woman, first off, any more than boats
or cars or anything else. And if it was a woman it would not be
an old mother but someone more like Janis Joplin or Angela Da-
vis. From now on, when someone says "Mother Nature," I'm—

"Time!" He walks around to collect our papers and smiles
when he sees the block of text on my page, taking credit for it
in some way, which I should have anticipated but I was thinking that I was writing something that he couldn't even have
an opinion about. Ha. He can have an opinion about anything. I sneer back at him.

After the Rasmatazz, we go downstairs for lunch: chicken
chow mein. It's mostly celery, but no one minds because of the
crunchy noodles they put out with it. Beth and I sit together and, after speed-eating for five minutes, she says to me, "I
think he knows."

"Knows what?"

"About my condition." She says this sooo dramatically, as
though she's a character in a soap opera, and then she cracks
up. I laugh along but not full out. I can sense she's about to
reveal something I didn't see coming, and that is my least favorite thing on earth.

"But what?" I finally ask her. "What are you talking about?"

"Let's do a test. Look at what I'm wearing and see if you can
figure it out."

Since when do I care what she's wearing? For the record, it's
a white, man-tailored shirt that's huge on her, and pink corduroy bell-bottoms. I see Beth every day and I've never seen
the pants before but she gets a lot of new clothes so that's not

particularly weird. The pants are the kind with patch pockets on the front and back and a high waist—sailor bells—and I wish I had some like that but my wardrobe is only what I can order from Sears or find at A&S. It's hard even finding blue jeans that fit me and I got stuck with Wranglers even though everyone else is wearing Levi's or Lee Riders. Anyway, Beth is wearing pink pants.

"New pants?"

"Well, yeah, but that's not the point. I guess he is kind of perceptive because *he* got it right away."

Now she's openly baiting me. I scan the lunchroom, looking at what everyone else is wearing for some kind of clue.

"HINT: It feels like rocks."

"Your period??" "It feels like rocks" is what Janie told Harriet in *The Long Secret*, which Beth gave me for my birthday in fifth grade and is still my second-favorite book of all time.

"A-duh!" We both laugh because of the way Beth says that phrase. She makes her upper lip stick out and crosses her eyes. But while I'm laughing a weird thought comes into my head out of nowhere: Beth's naked body. She's still a girl, not a woman, but with breasts and pubes and everything I don't yet have. The thought embarrasses me.

"My mother was so funny yesterday," I say, even though my mother is never funny. "I was playing Laura Nyro and she was trying to dance along with 'Stoned Soul Picnic.' She doesn't have a single ounce of natural rhythm."

Beth nods and continues her story. "He comes up behind me this morning and says, 'Don't worry, no one else can tell.'"

"Ew!"

"I know, but isn't that kind of crazy? He deduced it that I was covering up the bulge with the long shirt, and the pink pants are in case I leak."

"What bulge?"

"From the pad, stupid."

"You're wearing a sanitary napkin?"

"What else would I be wearing?"

"My mother bought me Tampax," I say, bragging. "She put them in my bathroom so we don't even have to discuss it when it happens." I thought this was extremely cool of her but Beth's face is perplexed.

"But you're a virgin," she says.

"And you're not?"

"You can't use tampons if you're a virgin."

"You can too . . ." As soon as the words are out of my mouth I begin to doubt myself. What do I actually know about any of this? Thankfully, she changes the subject. "Do you want to come with me to Loehmann's next weekend?"

I've never been to Loehmann's but I know what it is, more or less. I have no money to spend and no excuse for buying any new clothes but I want to go where Beth goes.

"How much money would I need?"

"How should I know? It depends on what you buy."

"How much will you bring?"

"Sometimes you're such a blockhead. Obviously, my mother buys my clothes for me. I have no idea. Ask your mother."

I make an appropriate face—she remembers who my mother is.

"Okay, bring a hundred dollars."

This would be almost funny except she doesn't appear to be joking. I've never even seen a hundred dollars. That would be like five years' worth of my allowance, and the most I've ever managed to save of that was enough to buy *The White Album*.

For dessert there is prune whip, which no one would dare eat.

7

Naomi

We were on the stoop with a bunch of the girls and I said one of them should come on up-stairs; she looked like she needed to lie down. I think it was Amelia. Chicken pox was going around. I said it out loud, like it was normal, because to me it was, but Bob grabbed me by the arm and took me inside right then and roared at me in a voice I'd not ever heard before: What was I thinking? How could I be so naïve? I know now that I was threatening his whole world, his master plan, but at the time I was blindsided. "She needs to lie down," I told him. "There's clean sheets," I said, thinking he was upset because I was go-ing to let her see our slovenly ways.

A year later, we had girls upstairs all the time. Girls get-ting their periods for the first time—I put them to bed with some whiskey and a hot water bottle like I was taught. Girls who were sleepy, or who needed a shower, and, eventually, girls who were going to get their picture taken, to "model." There were so many reasons to go upstairs, after a while, it's a wonder we ever sat in the kitchen. But we did that, too. One girl would be upstairs with Bob and I'd be downstairs with the others doing macramé or tie-dye, or baking cookies. They loved me because I never said much, and I told them they were beautiful, too.

I didn't even know what "ironic" meant then. Or maybe I did and I just let Bob tell me I didn't. I preferred to let him tell me what was what, because then it couldn't be all my fault. But in my heart I knew that it was: I'd given him the idea the day we met—before we mounted Babe the Blue Ox and rode off yonder. I myself was only fifteen years old when we sat behind Wilson's Café and I told him how I grew up. And on that day, he listened so well.

8

Nora

I have just begun to unpack the Singer folder when the wall of my cubicle speaks. "Your phone was ringing," says invisible Ktanya, a fellow paralegal—if she'd gone to the Academy, she'd be a lawyer herself, but she went to Boys and Girls High so she's a fantastically well-dressed clerical instead. She has never spoken directly to me before so I guess my visit to Jocelyn's office has increased my social currency. For the first six weeks of my tenure, Ktanya's desk belonged to creepy Arthur, who spent his whole day attempting to control his wife by phone, in a whisper that was fully audible to me: "Isn't it time for you to get dressed?" "I told you not to go there." "What were you doing at The Gap?" Ktanya is usually all business—dresses like a lawyer on a TV show, takes notes on a laptop, unfailingly begins and ends all her phone conversations with cordialities that sound almost nineteenth century to me. I know she has a husband and a young daughter, although there are never any personal phone calls over there. No messes of any kind. I ring my voicemail but there is no message waiting.

The first thing I need to do with any new case is let opposing counsel know we are interested in settling. Although our group is called "Settlements," this is not an actual lawsuit. I only settle complaints and disputes of the sort that can be decided by a hearing officer rather than a judge or jury. The standard of proof at these hearings is low—a "preponderance of evidence"—and the hearing officer is not even a lawyer let alone a judge. The outcome of such a proceeding is therefore unpredictable for all concerned. Anyway, the text of my letter to Singer's lawyer is standard, saying, "I'm your contact point, let's talk"—but in formalese. I just need a few key facts to customize it; the teacher's name (Harold Singer) and the case number go in the subject line, but I have to unpack the various manila folders that are wedged into the accordion file for the rest. I've never heard of the law firm. It's on Leonard Street in Tribeca so probably on the small side—not one of those places whose whole portfolio is suing the school system. The attorney's name is Elizabeth Cohen—the number of Beth Cohens in the world approaches the infinite, I sometimes think. My Beth married a Silicon Valley guy in 1980-something, and certainly showed no signs of becoming a lawyer. *Au contraire, Pierre*, as we used to say.

As Jocelyn mentioned, Harold Singer has been caught before but—like everything else at the ED—it's not really that simple. Sorting through the contents of the accordion file, I find the earlier case: Singer was charged with sexual impropriety but the hearing officer found in his favor. The full decision is too boring to bother reading but I scan it and am struck by the name of the girl in question, Elodie Cascarelli, who is represented by a few choice quotes:

I guess you could say he was "personal" with me.

Yes, I saw him outside of school a few times. So what?

He has a way of talking that lets you know you're important to him.

In the current case, my case, the victim isn't even named. The only people who seem certain Singer's done something wrong are one of his colleagues and another girl in the same classroom. There's a letter of reference from one of his professors from Teachers College, who calls him "gifted" and "dedicated." There's also a Letter to File from a former colleague, who calls him "one of the most inspiring and inventive young teachers I have ever met." His girlfriend? No, she says "in all my years of teaching"—so Singer is a charmer of middle-aged ladies, as well. Great.

The summary report of the city's special investigator is in all caps and exhausting to read—does he realize he's screaming? The upshot is that the principal told Singer, in writing, that he was not to spend time alone with female students in any capacity, and he was subsequently written up three times for disobeying: He offered homework help ("I didn't realize I was barred from helping my students") and he walked a girl to the subway after dark ("It was on my way, and we were in the middle of a conversation about the book she was reading; it didn't occur to me to cut her off mid-sentence"). The third incident involves such a grammatically tortured explanation of the configuration of the cafeteria entrance (somehow Singer and a student had been "alone" there) that I can't even follow it, despite reading it twice. I wonder if its all-caps author gets paid the same shit salary as me.

Anyway, Harold Singer is officially accused of insubordination—disobeying his principal—because there was no proof of sexual misconduct and the girl herself has not come forward. Nevertheless, if the hearing officer finds him guilty, he could lose not only his job but his pension—and for a teacher well into the third decade of his career, that's serious money, not to mention health insurance, for life.

In the absence of a photo of the guy, I find that I am picturing Bob Rasmussen whenever I read "Harold Singer." Rasmussen also never failed to have an answer to every question—a logical (though sometimes invented) explanation—and he, too, was free with his righteous indignation. Not that I ever saw him accused of doing anything wrong by a grown-up. Of course, in 1971 there was a lot more leeway for a guy like him, and at a school like the suffragette-founded Young Ladies' Academy of Brooklyn (where we didn't even have a dress code and sang "This Land is Your Land" instead of the national anthem every day) his colleagues seemed to view him as occasionally arrogant and irritating but nothing worse. I once heard our headmistress refer to him as "a lovable rake."

I hunt up the spreadsheet of comparable cases on our shared drive to find out exactly what facts I'll need to feed it in order to generate a settlement offer. The column headings are: Respondent's Age, Hire Date, Current Salary, Strength (which means "of our case"), and Severity (which must mean "of the offense"). How do I measure that? It's not a legal matter; no one saw anything. Technically his offense was disobeying his principal. Big deal.

This is typical of my job. There's no real training; they just give you the regs to read and a bunch of cases that have been written up for law journals or whatever and because you're smart and well-meaning—or were trained as an attorney in Kenya, or dropped out of law school—it is assumed that you will figure it out. And I do, but often the hard way.

The basic facts should be in the paperwork—sometimes they are: there's a cover sheet that someone is supposed to fill in before the case gets to the Settlement unit—but I can't find one in the Singer accordion file. I should just be able to look up the guy's personnel file somewhere on the computer network and get, for example, his hire date, but no, this requires a records request, a paper trail. I have to write a polite and correctly formatted email to a lady named Shonda Deville in the Manifest Records Unit, who replies with a polite, five-sentence email, the gist of which is: "Your request has been received." She has a quote from Dr. Martin Luther King underneath her cursive-font signature. After a week (but not sooner) I can follow up with another email and, five days later, an apologetic phone call, but even then I never find out whether there are a hundred requests ahead of mine, or ten, or a thousand. When something is "on for hearing" in a few days like this case, I can add a boilerplate first paragraph requesting expedited handling but even then—what if Shonda is sick or on vacation? What if she has trouble finding the records—sometimes she has to resort to looking up paper files and must, herself, send a records request to the storage facility in Staten Island, and on and on. I write my request and set myself a reminder to follow up first thing in the morning. And although it is probably the least efficient way to find anything, I return to the accordion file and start to read.

It surprises me that Singer went to Teachers College—in other words, he must have been smart and enthusiastic and all that once upon a time. TC is hard to get into, not to mention expensive. He could have gotten a job in a private school or out in the suburbs—so he is also an idealist of some sort. I guess he is the kind of pervert who thinks he is rescuing his victims from ignorance and poverty—but then how'd he end up at the Children's City School in Murray Hill? It's one of those school-within-a-schools that the ED started doing a few years ago—along with magnet schools, and outdoor schools, and charter schools, and anything else that might counter the overall impression of failure and despair. Anyway, Singer must be good at his job or they wouldn't have hired him in the first place. Of course, there's no reason a pedophile can't also be a good teacher. I learned that from Rasmussen.

9
Nora

Lunch is a confusing time of day for me. The apartment is a fifteen-minute walk, so clearly I *should* go home. No one here expects me to work through lunch, and even if I did, it wouldn't count—I wouldn't get paid for the time—but if I come back more than two minutes late, they dock my check and, after three lates, there's some kind of probation or warning, so mostly I stay close. But all I can really get to eat in the immediate neighborhood is a burger, pizza, or "street meat." Obviously, I should bring a sandwich and I have resolved to do this numerous times, but making myself lunch at eight in the morning is apparently beyond my capabilities as a human being. I'm sure that's related to the fact that my mother never mastered that skill, either, and used to send me to grade school with atrocities like a jar of olives or a can of sardines—this was before the invention of the Lunchable. Maybe that's part of why I wound up at the Academy. They served a hot lunch every day and every girl was expected to sit down and eat it.

Anyway, it's twelve thirty, I'm so hungry I could plotz, and I'm sitting immobile at my desk when my cell phone starts ringing in my bag, in the desk drawer. I don't even keep it on my desk, because since moving back to Brooklyn and starting this job I have been as bad at keeping up my friendships as I have at making myself lunch. It's an unfamiliar 718 number, but I've gone to the trouble of getting the thing out so I answer it.

"Is this Eleanor?" says a male voice. No one has ever called me Eleanor. I can't even imagine who would know that it's my real name.

"Yes," I say, with some discomfort.

"I think I have your cat," he says. "I got your number from Sammy."

It takes me a second but I realize he means Sami, the man who owns Pets Emporium on Montague Street, and who knows everyone and everything in Brooklyn Heights. And because Sami lets me pay for cat food with checks that he often has to hold onto until payday, he has read my phone number off of one of them, along with the name printed above it, to this guy. I told Sami to keep an eye out for Tin Man when he first failed to come home.

"Where are you?" I ask my caller.

"Poplar Street," he says. If Tin Man is in the neighborhood, he should have come home by now. He knows the way. So I am unbalanced by this news.

"Is he okay?"

"He's fine. A little skinny, but fine."

"Where did you find him?"

"The old playground on Columbia Heights."

"Squibb Park? But it's closed. The entrance is all boarded up."

"Not to cats, obviously."

"And you were there looking for cats?" The old playground has not had playground equipment in it for some time, maybe since I was a kid when it had sprinklers and we would roller skate down the long ramp that led into the park, gathering speed until we thought we might career right off the thing and into the river. Impossible, of course, but that's my memory. Also, there were tough kids there—maybe from Farragut, the projects? But of course the adjoining neighborhood is no longer a wasteland, it's DUMBO—full of wealthy white people living in converted industrial spaces.

"I heard there was a cat down there so I went over the other night with some tuna."

He's one of those cat-rescue people. I'm always surprised that there are men in that cohort. "Are you home now?" I ask. "Can I come get him?"

This is a terrible idea because I can't come back to the office with my cat, and anyway he's heavy and I have no carrier, but now that I have taken in the possibility that he is alive, and nearby, I want him back desperately. In the past year, that cat has become my best friend, my boon companion. At times, I've slept holding his fucking paw.

"I have to leave at four thirty," he says. "Sixty Poplar. Apartment three."

"I'll be there," I say. "Probably not until four, but I'll be there."

I hang up and realize I didn't even get the guy's name. He knows Sami, and he's a cat rescuer so he's probably not a murderer/rapist, but it hits me that I've just agreed to go alone to the apartment of a man I've never met at a time of day when, if I disappeared, no one would miss me until tomorrow morning at work. (José the doorman doesn't keep track of my comings and goings, although he does continue to ask after the cat—my mother must have been a good tipper.)

I go down to the newsstand in the lobby and buy a Styrofoam bowl of Special K, a banana, and a mini milk, which I scarf down at my desk. I'll still be ninety minutes short if I leave at three thirty, but if I can get this offer done before then, maybe Jocelyn will let me take it as sick leave or something. I trash the remains of my lunch and go back to the spreadsheet, but after staring at it for another minute or two, I decide to follow Jocelyn's original instructions: just offer.

I open my email and pull up the offer letter template. My normal procedure is to start with an obscenely low number and see what happens—the used-car-buying approach to justice. I take pleasure in typing the phrase "termination without severance or other ensuing benefits"—I guess I really am a bureaucrat. But before I can save and send the thing, an email message arrives and the transparent box that previews its contents informs me that it's from Elizabeth Cohen, the guy's attorney, apparently responding to the "here I am" email I sent earlier. I'm about to read it when I realize someone is hovering at the entrance to my cube. Two people, actually: Jocelyn and one of the attorneys, a large woman in a tight, flowered dress. For some reason, I feel as though I have been caught in a guilty act. Both women say, "Hi," simultaneously when I look up at them.

Jocelyn says, "This is Alessandro, she works in appeals. She's my go-to for kiddie sex stuff."

Alessandro, to my amazement, hoots with laughter while grabbing my boss's arm—as though Jocelyn's a normal human being!

"You are too much!" she says, and then to me, "Hi, I'm Gina."

We shake hands.

"Anyway," says Jocelyn, "I realize I threw you in the dark end of the pool, deep end, whatever, shut up Alessandro, and this one can probably help you out. End of speech." She turns and leaves after a strange, ceremonial nod. Gina steps inside my cube and leans her butt on the desktop.

"Isn't she a kick?" she says of Jocelyn.

"It hadn't occurred to me to view her as anything other than an authority figure," I say, which is true, but sounds so stiff and schoolmarmish that I want immediately to start over. I like Gina, I realize. She's funny. This place needs funny so badly it should be our motto: "New York City Education Department: Please tell us a joke!"

"So tell me what you've got," says Gina. I fill her in. She asks good questions. When I finish, I expect her to issue a solution of some sort but she just nods and waits.

"What should I do?" I say, finally.

"Sounds like you have a strategy," she says. "Lowball, right? You don't have time to really dig in and find your backup singers."

"What do you mean?"

"Well, if I were taking this to hearing on Monday—which I couldn't even if I wanted to—but if I was, what I'd need are witnesses. The other side's going to have the guy's mother and his sister and the homeless dude he gives dollars to all there to convince the hearing officer that he's just a good guy who bends the rules a little. The only way to play that off is to have a parade of girls saying he's a perv, even if he never touched them. So I would basically get all his class rosters and start calling."

"You can do that?"

"Right, I don't think you have access to that stuff. And even if you did, it takes forever to pull the records. And then, nine times out of ten, the family doesn't want the girl to testify: they think they're protecting her. Like even just talking about sex is dirty—and as though that pathetic little hearing room was open court. I don't think anybody realizes till they get there that it's more like a mechanic's waiting room than *bum-pum*. Right?"

I nod. It takes me a second to understand that the two-note sound *bum-pum* means the TV franchise *Law and Order* but when I do, I can't help but smile. I find this woman so interesting—I've passed her in the halls dozens of times, and based entirely on the flowered dresses and her choice of profession, I'd assumed she was from a different planet than mine. Of course, I assume that about everyone—it's something I need to work on.

"I don't know why people don't see that getting your daughter on record against a real creep *is* keeping her safe, not to mention teaching her to stand up for herself. Nobody wants to consider how this stuff tends to come back and haunt you later on, and how crap the statute of limitations is in New York."

I remember this coming up on that Facebook thread about Rasmussen that appeared last year, but I never really took in the details. "How crap is it?"

"If you don't start proceedings by the time you're twenty-three, tough luck."

I think about myself at twenty-three—I was still under multiple delusions about the transformative power of growing up. I don't think I started really noticing how much the stuff with Rasmussen had affected me until I was in my forties.

"I had a teacher like this guy," I say to Gina.

"He raped you?" she asks.

"Some of my friends. I almost went on a camping trip where it probably would have been me, too, but I changed my mind at the last minute."

"Smart kid," says Gina, but she looks at her watch and I realize she needs to go, and I need to get back on this thing.

"Thanks so much," I say. And she says, "Any time."

I have forgotten all about the email I was about to read, but when I wake up my monitor, there it is:

Dear Ms. Buchbinder,

Thank you for your correspondence in the matter of Harold Singer. As you know, the hearing is set for Monday so time is of the essence. The latest we can accept an offer for consideration would be tomorrow at noon.

Sincerely,

Elizabeth Cohen

P.S. I knew a Nora Buchbinder a long time ago, in Brooklyn Heights. Is that you?

10
Nora

At the end of the summer between seventh and eighth grades, Beth and I swore we would never, ever, ever become members of Rasmussen's cult. (We didn't have the concept of "cult" yet—this was pre-Moonies—but we knew that there was something more than nicknames that bound together the eighth-grade girls every year.) We were in Beth's finished basement—a large wood-paneled room decorated with caricatures of her parents drawn at Grossinger's Resort: giant-headed, tooth-heavy creatures skiing, golfing, riding on a speedboat. We sat at the bamboo-edged wet bar, a piece of sky-blue American Tourister hand luggage open on the counter between us. The case contained Beth's mother's castoff makeup collection and had a mirror mounted inside its lid. In my mind its contents present a perfect still life, a pile of very specific detritus that I can see as if it were a photograph.

"Do you think they actually do stuff with him?" Beth asked me. I didn't have to ask who "they" or "him" were, even though we'd been actively recapping our respective summer vacations until that very second. "Gross me out!" I'm sure I responded, and I'm sure we giggled, because that was what we mostly did together, in and out of school. Beth had orange lipstick on her teeth. I watched her prime a cake of eyeliner with spit. I remember the sensation of having my eyelids painted, knowing the cool slickness was saliva but not minding, really. "You should wear this to school," she told me. I probably said, "When chickens have teeth," because that was one of our running jokes—a reference to the time in sixth grade when Beth had attempted to comment on an overly obvious plot turn in *Encyclopedia Brown* by rhetorically asking, "I mean, is the Pope Jewish?" Then we played Would You Rather.

Touch Bob Rasmussen's penis or eat a raw hamburger?

Let Bob Rasmussen put his tongue in your mouth or spend a day locked in the first-floor broom closet with Mrs. Cashin's farts?

Broom closet, I said, but it wasn't necessarily true. The tongue thing would only last a second and I would kind of like to know what that feels like, although it would have to be over as soon as I said so. The closet would be hard for me, even fart-free. I get claustrophobic.

Beth and I often argued. In retrospect, the subject seemed to have always been a version of the same thing: what was the truth and which one of us understood it? Once, in Beth's recently redecorated bedroom (which featured an "Expressionist" painting that precisely matched the colors in the olive-, turquoise-, and navy-checkered bedspreads), I pointed out that her new wood paneling was not real. Beth would more readily have accepted that the earth was flat. I didn't know the term "particle board," but I could see that the wood grain pattern repeated itself, and was printed on the surface rather than integral to it—I have always looked at things a little too closely. Another time, we stopped speaking for two days over a magazine ad for blonde hair dye, which showed a woman beside a "candid" photo of her supposed younger self, with identical locks. Beth believed this to be a real childhood photo of the model as a young woman; I was outraged by her naïveté. Later, we had an ongoing debate over whether or not Rasmussen "came from money." He'd told our class that his family had been on food stamps, to illustrate that people's assumptions about who was on welfare were racist and misguided. Beth said this meant he was "working class." I said that was impossible, because he freely admitted that he'd gone to boarding school; she said he could have been on scholarship. And so on.

Later, the night of the pre-Rasmussen sleepover, lying in the twin beds in Beth's bedroom with the lights out, we returned to the subject of our new teacher and our classmates and who would, and who wouldn't, or might, and whether the girls from previous years really were having sex or just acting like they were.

"I can imagine second base, maybe."

"I think further," said Beth.

"Why?"

"How should I know why? I'm not doing it."

"I meant, why do *you* think that they go further?" I waited a really long time for her to answer. I could tell she had something to say if she could figure out how to say it.

"I saw them in the art room once. Him and Tamsin. He had his hands in her pants."

"Both hands? Did they see you?"

"No."

"That's so barfy!"

"Barfamatic!"

"I would never even let him touch me on the arm," I said.

"Not even on the toe!"

"And if he gives me a stupid nickname I'll tell him to shove it."

"Did I ever tell you he was my teacher in third grade?"

"What?" I looked at her with real horror. How could she have withheld this fact?

"Mrs. Stark had her baby early and he subbed. Just for like a month."

"You never said that. That you knew him already."

"It was third grade!"

"So, have you been to his house?"

"Yeah. Once."

"Does he really have a waterbed?"

"Nora! I didn't go in their bedroom! It was the whole class. We did folk singing."

"But you never would, would you? Go in his bedroom?"

"You're so gross. Of course not."

"Let's make a pact."

"Okay, no blood though."

So it was a spit-swear—a step up from a double-dog-dare-you, but inviolable in my eyes. I still don't really understand why I had to banish her so completely when she broke it, but banish her I did. And I guess I now have an opportunity to make up for that.

11
Bob

From: bear@nyc.rr.com
To: PBJ@nyc.rr.com
Date sent: Feb 19 2009 12:45 PM MST
Subject: Laramie

Peanut,

My daughter's church is one of those yellow brick enormities. No one puts up buildings that crappy anymore, even on college campuses. At Antioch, my freshman dorm looked like that, but at least it didn't have the sad, inevitable sign out front—the quote must have sounded better in Aramaic. It's from Corinthians, abbreviated 1 COR: "Know ye not that a little leaven leaveneth the whole lump?" Here I am, the unleavened lump, live and in person. I parked across the street like some stalker or surveillance expert. I got there at eight, even though the service started at nine, just in case they tried to give me the slip. Really, I had that thought. Last night was rough.

I see them, because I see him. Doria I wouldn't have recognized because she's fat. I get out of the car and cross the street, waving. She doesn't recognize me, either. I call out, "Pumpkin!" which I realize is all wrong the moment it escapes my lips. At eight, even ten, "Pumpkin" was adorable and round, but at forty-two it's inappropriate and depressing. So I call her by her name and realize how long it's been since I've done so. She turns stiffly, holding tight to Ray's hand, and then waves back, and then freezes. As we meet at the curb, she nods and introduces her husband. We shake hands and arrange to meet at Shoney's for breakfast. She gives me excellent directions.

Things are awkward at the coffee shop. Doria fidgets with her silverware and seems self-conscious about ordering a Diet Coke. The waitress reminds her that it's bottomless, which is I'm sure what she says to every customer but I flinch at the word as though it's some kind of inside joke. Despite her new heft, Doria's still wearing her hair in a long braid like the ones she and Naomi both had in the seventies. It looks wrong on her and even wronger when Ray holds onto the end of it while she's talking, like a microphone he might decide to speak into at any moment. Not to disparage—he loves my daughter. He listens to everything she says with his whole body, as though it's important to suck up every inference. He has the instant smile of a four-year-old. I desperately want him to leave us alone but, instead, Doria excuses herself. I watch the braid swaying against her turquoise sweatshirt as she trundles off. I can't believe my little girl is in there somewhere.

Then Ray says, "Are you sure your regrets are the same as hers?"

"Say again?"

"You're here to 'make amends' right? But it's *except when to do so would injure them or others*. I think the kindest thing you can do for Doria, now, is to follow her lead."

"I'm not really a step follower," I say, defensively, as though it makes me some kind of maverick. He's got a fuckload of nerve assuming he knows why I'm here, especially since he's right. And I realize this is exactly why she married a blind black dude. His moral high ground is so far up that the oxygen masks are about to drop. All I can do is nod and put it all back in the box in my head: the fantasy of forgiveness, or even of just getting past Step Fucking Nine.

When Doria gets back, she can tell the mood has changed so she starts prattling on about the jazz choir she's in and how much I would appreciate their arrangement of "High Flyin' Bird," which is a song title I can't even place until a hundred miles later, when I find myself singing it. Havens's *Mixed Bag* was Naomi's favorite record for a long time when the kids were little. Is that what she remembers? Anyway, after that she throws me a curveball: Have you seen Archer?

"No."

"Well I have," says Doria.

"Did he know you?"

"Hard to say. I don't think so." But what I hear is *whether or not he can recognize us is beside the point, he's your fucking son*. I'm sure I look guilty as hell, because I am, and she sees that: "Remember when we used to go visit your dad in Connecticut? I used to say I was carsick, or allergic to the pillows, or afraid of the bunk beds . . . you never let me get away with any of it."

Of course, I start thinking that her fear of Percy was founded on something far worse. She sees me biting my nails and says, "That wasn't why." And I should hug her for reading my mind, for protecting her poor old dad from his own worst thoughts but those thoughts, once aroused, aren't easily dismissed and while I'm supposed to be asking follow-up questions about my son, all I can think about is my father. Did he touch her? A feeling of rage and disgust overwhelms me and I'm afraid I will throw a chair, or roar like a beast, or tear the head off the first old white man I see—which would of course be my own self. I stare out the window at nothing, instead.

"Really, Dad," she says. "Nothing like that. I just disliked him. It's not hereditary!"

"What went wrong with your brother, then?"

"There was no indication of that." She is vehement.

"I'd call trying to blow your own head off an indication," I say, and Ray says, "More likely rage than guilt. Suicides want to hurt someone close."

"But there wasn't anyone close to him to hurt," I say, and they both face me in utter dismay. Ray, who doesn't know how to mask his emotions, is actually showing me something closer to disgust. They don't say Naomi's name, but I hear it of course. She was so close she was right there. And then she wasn't.

Really only to change the subject, I get the name of the state hospital where Archer is now, outside Denver. Doria says she thinks it would be good for me to see him, and all I can think of is "Good for who?" because my son will never be twenty-one, or independent, or a man at the wheel of his own car, on this two-lane blacktop, going anywhere fast.

I'm headed back to the badlands before noon, pedal to the metal, sobbing and drooling like an old man. The car's due back in Phoenix but I can't seem to point it in the right direction. I say out loud at one point, "Go home, you idiot," but I don't. And I call you and call you, Peanut, but you don't answer your phone.

12
Nora

I read Beth's email again. I google "Elizabeth Cohen, JD, NYC," and there she is, on a "Who We Are" page. Her hair is blondish now and it looks like maybe she had a nose job, but it's unmistakably my Beth. It's like looking in some kind of funhouse mirror that compiles the past and the future—well, the present: this is the age we actually are now. I haven't seen her since the year we went off to college—we'd stayed in touch through high school but she was at Packer and I was at Music & Art and our worlds were already diverging: she was disco and I was Grateful Dead. I heard from her when she got married—ridiculously early, it seemed to me then, ardent feminist that I was—and since then I've been storing mental pictures of her in Los Altos or Milpitas or wherever it was, entertaining in hostess pajamas and going to Little League games, married to her boring dude-with-money who I viewed with contempt in 1983 but now totally understand. I should have married a Wall Street guy—although in fifty-two years of New York City life, I've barely even met one.

I read her bio and learn that she got her law degree in 2001—from Pace! She's only been at the firm since 2003 and it doesn't say what she did before. It's not clear if she has a specialty. I wonder if she took Singer on for some reason other than being assigned the case. Maybe he's a friend? I mean, why else would she be defending a pedophile? But the whole thing is confusing—clearly she's been back in New York since the nineties, at least. How many times have I passed her on the street or just missed her in the mammogram waiting room, the ticket-holders line at the Angelika? Clearly she never looked for me. I guess she stayed mad—for dropping her, which I did. She wrote me a desperate-sounding letter during our freshman year at college and I never wrote back. Her crisis might even have been about Rasmussen. Or maybe it wasn't. I just remember that she seemed to be falling apart, and I didn't know how to deal with it. In truth I was still mad at her for breaking our pact.

At Loehmann's, Beth is trying on an outfit: palazzo pants (which are basically bell-bottoms so wide that they are not even pants anymore) and a matching middy blouse. What matches is the paisley trim around the edges and the tie around the neck, which are the same pattern as the pants. I think she looks ridiculous but she is enchanted with herself. She starts doing the Pony, and then that other weird shivering dance move that she does, which I think is supposed to make her tits ripple but just makes the pant legs start to undulate. I take a mental snapshot of her in mid-writhe.

"Check it out!" she says. I hate it when she says that, because she picked it up from Bob.

"Cool," I say. I can hear that some of the other women in the communal dressing room have mixed feelings about the dancing teenager in their midst.

"It's between this and the purple mini-dress," she says. "What about you, are you getting that?"

I am wearing a short-sleeved white dress made out of the fattest-wale corduroy I have ever seen—it's like velvet. I wouldn't have expected it to look very good on me—I picked it out because of the fabric—but it does. Also, it has pockets, and when I look at myself in the mirror with my hands in them and my hair swept over one shoulder, I look like a model, for some reason. On the other hand, it costs seventy-five dollars.

"Where would I wear it?" I ask Beth.

"Anywhere. It's a casual look."

"Yeah, but not school, and it's not like I go to the theater or out to dinner or anything."

"On a date."

"Yeah, right."

The woman standing closest to us, who is trying on a hideous red pantsuit, says, "You're not getting any taller. You'll have that in your wardrobe for years."

"Unlike the palazzo sailor outfit," I add.

"Exactly," says the lady.

For some reason, I act like I'm going to buy the dress. I carry it with me when we go back out into the fray, and I still have it when I follow Beth over to the line at the register. In my head I am debating whether to ask her if I can borrow the money and then wondering how I would ever pay it back. But when they finish ringing up Beth's things (she also got a peasant top made out of crumpled-looking flowered chiffon and a purple Borsalino hat) she turns around and holds her hand out for my dress and I give it to her. She can see the look of panic in my eyes. "To my bat mitzvah, stupid," she says.

"You're . . . ?" But she is back with the cashier, counting hundreds and fifties out of the envelope her mother gave her.

It has her father's return address: Stanley Cohen, MD. He's a cardiologist. I've never met him because every time I've been at their house he's been either at work or asleep in his Barcalounger, in front of the TV.

Beth hands me a brown paper shopping bag. This place doesn't even have its name on the shopping bags—that is so weird. "March twelfth," she says, "at the beach club in Margate." I have never heard of Margate and I have no idea why you would have your big swinging party in a beach cabana in March but that's not even the part that's confusing me most.

"So, don't you have to go to Hebrew school and everything?"

"I do go to Hebrew school."

"You do not."

"I do, too! What makes you think you know everything?"

We're standing inside waiting for her mother because it's late November and suddenly cold out, but now she is pushing through the doors to the street. I follow.

"Because you're my best friend since fifth grade?"

"Yeah, well, I guess you never asked what I was doing on Saturday mornings between nine and eleven."

That's true. I assumed she was watching cartoons, like everyone else in the universe. "But you never even talk about it. I mean, don't you have friends there? Aren't there boys?"

"Yes and yes."

"And you never even mentioned them?" She has stopped at the corner and is peering into the traffic coming down Flatbush Avenue. We could basically walk to her house from here, or take the 41 bus.

"I did so mention them. Where do you think I met David?" David was a guy that Beth had made out with over the summer. "Where do you think I learned to Frug, and to French kiss? Not in folk dancing class."

"Where's your mom coming from?"

"Tennis lesson."

"I'm freezing."

"The dress is on me." Then she turns to me, giving me the Beth Eyeball. "In return for your sworn secrecy."

"You don't have to buy me a dress to get me to keep a secret!"

"Shut up and ask me what the secret is." She is gleeful, but trying to hide it.

"What's the secret?"

"I'm going to have sex with Rasmussen."

I look at her with all the "WHAT?" I can muster. She looks back without any sign of backing down. "Like, 'someday'? Is that what you mean?"

"Next Thursday."

The expression on my face must be hilarious, because she laughs at me, but I still want answers. "You have a date to lose your virginity with our teacher?"

"No, I have a date to go over to his house after school and get help on my report. As soon as he shuts the door, I'm going to take off my shirt."

Beth does have breasts, it's true. They stand up straight and high, like dog snouts—in a photograph, they would be more humorous than sexy—but she seems to think she will seduce him instantly.

"Why?" I say, wishing Mrs. Cohen would show up already, because that would end this conversation.

"Because I want to. I think about it constantly."

I watch two buses pass right behind one another. We could be on one of them. But no.

"What about our pact?" I say, finally.

"The pact was immature. I had no idea I was going to feel this way, obviously."

"I don't think it was immature, I think it was sensible. I mean, he's married, for one thing."

"We didn't make the pact because he's married, we made it because we thought he was gross. I don't think that anymore."

I don't have a counter to that one and anyway Beth's mother's car pulls up—a blue Ford station wagon with Gene McCarthy daisy stickers on the fake wood panel. Roberta is wearing huge sunglasses and has an unlit cigarette in her mouth. She reaches for the lighter before she turns to us and says, "Get in," though we can't really hear her through the window.

"Remember, I bought you the dress," says Beth, getting into the car. I get in beside her and look out the window as we drive. All I can think about is the down-pointing arrow of orange hair I can see on his belly when Rasmussen raises his arms and his T-shirt lifts up. I would rather think about anything in the world than our teacher's naked body—concentration camps, nuclear war, anything.

On Thursday afternoons we had "electives" at the Academy. You could take typing, music appreciation, or photography, which was taught by Bob Rasmussen. I'd gone for typing in the fall but in the spring my envy of the girls with cameras around their necks won out over my mistrust of our teacher.

Had I seen the movie *Blow-Up* or just the photos of topless Vanessa Redgrave? In any case, I wanted to be *her*. The dark-room was in the attic of the Academy building—larger than a closet but quite small with twelve girls and a large adult man crammed into it. He showed us the procedures for loading and developing film as a group, then sent us out to document our lives. At first, I took a lot of pictures of fire hydrants and subway cars in order to appear gritty—my life seemed not worth documenting. But one day, scanning around my grand-father's apartment, I realized that everything looked different through the lens; old clothes, piles of books, cracked paint on the windowsills, everything. The camera itself became a fetish object, the *chunk* sound of the shutter so satisfying! Like bit-ing off pieces of life.

When it came time to print my selects, Rasmussen pro-vided individual instruction. Thus there was every legitimate reason for him to stand behind me and use both his hands to direct mine as I adjusted the size and focus of the enlarger's projected image, and also as I set each fresh sheet of paper in the metal frame, then exposed it while counting aloud, and then slid it in and out of the three chemical baths with bam-boo tongs. It made sense to stand that way, in the red safe-ty light. And when he made me flinch with a quick tickle or nudge, he clearly demonstrated that my tension was silly—that I was being uptight.

My desire came out of nowhere. Did I actually want him to touch me? Was leaning into me even really "touching" me? What about massaging my belly? That couldn't have been okay. I told him to stop.

"Why, doesn't it feel good?"

"No," I said. I must have said no, because he stopped—and that was as strange or stranger than the smells of hypo and fixer, the alchemy of seeing the previous week's glimpsed moments swimming back into view, becoming facts. I still wonder if I was the only girl who refused him or if there was something else that separated me at that point, that made me unlike the others. Sometimes it feels like my life took a turn at that moment, that the volume got cranked on my sense of what was at risk when a man touched me, or tried to, and it never really got turned back down. Obviously, that was the last time I went into the darkroom.

13
Nora

I'm looking at Facebook, which I shouldn't be doing at work, but I am at a stuck place in the Singer case: I should make an offer now, but the reappearance of Beth has derailed my thinking. Instead, I scroll back and back in the Academy alumnae group and finally realize I need a better strategy to find what I'm looking for: the Rasmussen thread from last year, which I had then chosen to ignore—even after a group of my classmates formed in its aftermath, and Trina asked if I wanted to join their attempt at a lawsuit. I remembered thinking that Trina's was one of the voices that ran through the whole thread—skein? hairball? (It had gone on for days.) The person I thought was Trina had an obviously made-up screen name, which I now can't remember. So, who else was there? Daisy Kramer. I know she's one of my "friends" because I remember combing through her brother's bar mitzvah pictures from 1969 at some point. Luckily, Daisy is not much of a Facebooker, so I only have to go back a few pages to find what I'm looking for: "Daisy commented on a post in Academy Alumnae (Brooklyn Hts)." I click through.

Her comment is in the first third of the thread—late on the first day—and says, in its entirety: *What I learned in those days was to be very, extremely wary of leftish males with a cause.*

I scan the next few loosely connected comments:

—*Times were so different then, we thought free love was a political thing.*

—*And a girl who liked sex was called a "nymphomaniac." Remember that?*

—*Daisy, I once heard you refer to Rasmussen as a male chauvinist pig and I think I was somewhere near awestruck.*

—*I am sure there is an appropriate Woody Guthrie song that we should sing now.*

—*But R was the one who taught us to hear the irony in those songs. Sometimes I think I'm the only person in America who doesn't think This Land is Your Land is the same thing as Kumbaya.*

—*He manipulated all of us! When I hear bullshit like, well, it was a small price to pay for learning to think independently (this, of course, only from the un-raped), I am speechless.*

When this was all going on—something like 250 comments—it seemed to break Facebook. Text started showing up doubled and fragmented and the conversation got very out of sync. What was even weirder was that, because the participants were all good Academy girls, while talking about rape and molestation they were also writing things like: *You were the fastest runner in the school!* and *Say hi to your sister for me.*

I keep scrolling till get to the part I wanted to revisit: A girl who calls herself Zed says she believes Rasmussen must regret his deeds. *Maybe watching Doria become a teenager,* she theorizes, adding, *After all, he wasn't a monster to his kids.* A girl named Patty Hearst says she wrote to him once and he wrote back and said he was sorry and "in recovery." That one hits with a thunk. People apparently have a lot of mixed feelings about the language of twelve-step programs:

—WTF is in recovery? Is he accepting responsibility or not?

—You make it sound like he's the one who was harmed.

—Wait, there's a program for being a child molester? Why don't the cops just raid the meetings?

A former Academy teacher shows up and offers her memories of "when it all first came out": an emergency meeting of the school's board of directors after the summer van trip went awry.

—In answer to one of your questions above, there was no thought of calling the police. The girls' parents didn't want us to, and neither did the girls. One of them, Beth Cohen I think— Beth if you're out there please chime in—she yelled her head off at the headmistress. None of us knew how to respond. Why we were influenced by the histrionics of an obviously distraught eighth grader, I don't know. Now, that seems idiotic.

Beth never chimed in. Neither did Naomi—who seemed voiceless back when we were kids but was a source of fascinated speculation in the Facebook thread: *How did she live with herself? What did she tell her kids? Did she stay with him after the move to Vermont? After the kids were grown?* No one had any information about Naomi, at all.

In the late-night hours of the second day, between two and three a.m., Zed and Patty Hearst began carrying on a more intimate conversation, as though they were alone. Perhaps they were, at the time.

—I didnt have birth control. U?

—Were u pregnant??

—Yea, I had no idea it was rape then.

—Sometimes I forget I was her and feel like whatever and then I see his hands on me.

—He bit his nails.

—We made cookies after. In his house.

—I feel like no one believes it was real.

—I know. Like we imagined.

—It took so long to even talk about it. Even my husband.

—It's good that u told him tho.

—You have to tell the story until it can't hurt you anymore.

—Does that happen?

—I don't know.

—He taught me to write. Sometimes it still feels like he's in my head.

In my own head there is a photograph of Zed—for some reason, I think she is Tamsin, the one Bob liked to call "Christmas." Her long, wavy hair is obscuring most of her face and there is lamplight raking crosswise against the horizontal shadows of her ribs, making a kind of mesh pattern. He must have shown it to our whole class? Or maybe he showed it to me, that afternoon in the darkroom. In any case, it is the image that returns to me when I think of Rasmussen-as-rapist. It's a picture of a girl enmeshed, trapped, but believing herself to be a willing volunteer.

I open my home email account and hunt up last year's email from Trina—the one I never responded to. It says:

Hi, Nora,

It's been a while. I hope this email still works. Some of us are talking to a lawyer and we wondered if you wanted to be

part of that. I know you didn't think he harmed you, personally, last time we talked, but time changes things and anyway
I thought you might want to share your story.

I hit reply and write:

Sorry it's taken me so long to write back. I'm assuming you
went ahead with the lawyer—and I'd be curious to know
what's happening, if you feel like telling me. But the real reason I'm writing is that I'm wondering if you ever got in touch
with Beth Cohen, if she's part of your suit. I don't know if you
remember but she was my best friend.

Writing those last five words is strangely painful. I hit send.

When I first got Trina's email, I'd wanted to write back but
I kept getting caught up in the argument inside my head
about what actually happened to them, to me, to us, back at
the Academy. I've never stopped wondering whether I should
have blown the whistle somehow or prevented Beth from getting involved . . . or gone along on that van trip myself instead
of chickening out at the last minute.

I was still in college when there was that first big lawsuit at
Yale Law School, but I never made a connection between what
they were then calling "sexual harassment" and Rasmussen.
The Yale women argued that there was an unequal power
relationship, that their liaisons with their professors were
coerced even if they seemed consensual—because the men
had undue influence over their futures, their careers. At the
Academy, we hadn't gotten grades, and even if we had it
was middle school—we had no notion of "careers" beyond

the board game. And, I told my twenty-one-year-old self, Rasmussen had taught us things we would have never known otherwise—not just about sex but about music, and art, and writing, and politics. He hadn't taken advantage of us; we'd each had a choice. Some of us had even said no.

Then, in the mid-eighties I guess, there was another wave of stuff in the news and the concept of "harassment" got supplanted by the idea of "abuse": the McMartin preschool, another one in Massachusetts, allegations of satanic rituals, animal sacrifice, ceremonial bloodletting—

I read it all with deep fascination, as though the stories contained some key to understanding my own past, but they were about the rape of helpless children, not the seduction of teenagers. The girls in Rasmussen's class had been fully capable of desire and arousal. Fourteen is an age at which women have become wives and mothers for most of human history, after all. I'd been sexually active—at least in my head—since age six or eight: playing doctor with my friends, attempting to masturbate my cat, fantasizing about George Harrison . . . And on it went, the argument in my head. Stories continued to arise in the news, occasionally rumors would even surface about Rasmussen himself (that he was living in Vermont, that Naomi had left him), and I would return to the questions I couldn't ever resolve, year after year. Was Rasmussen a criminal? Was I harmed? Was Beth? Men will always desire girls in that maddening stage of beauty, and girls at that age are always over-ready to leave their parents and get on with life—that much seemed proven over and over. In any case, I am fine, unharmed, normal. My decisions have been my own decisions: I'm single because it's what I've chosen, not because I'm damaged. Then, my desk phone rings and my whole body jumps.

"Buchbinder," I answer.

"I knew it was you!"

It's Beth. I know this without hesitation. It's not like I was stalking her on Facebook but I guess in a way I was. Stalking our past. I am shaking.

"This is so weird," I say.

"I know."

"Are you calling about the case?"

"Let's get it out of the way, shall we?"

I'm relieved that she says this; I'm not sure I want to have the other conversation, the one about our lives since 1980. In comparison, the Singer case seems straightforward. I come out swinging:

"How can you defend a pedophile?"

"If he was a pervert, he'd be in jail by now, don't you think? After ten years of teaching? Everyone in the school system is a mandated reporter."

"But what if he's clever, like Rasmussen?"

"Jesus, I knew you'd go there. Get over it. It's a different world. You can't get away with shit like that anymore."

Her voice is older, a bit shaded, but I feel like I'm still bickering with my best friend from eighth grade.

"Six-month suspension," she adds. "You know you've got no case."

"If that's true then he'll be cleared at the hearing. Why are you so interested in settling?"

"He's been five months already waiting for this hearing and it's killing him. He's done. That's the whole point of the rubber room, right? To get people to quit rather than spend every day in a de facto psych ward? Harold's a great teacher, an idealist. Did you read his evals?"

I'm still trying to figure out what I should say next when she ups her offer:

"Okay, one-year suspension and a penalty, ten thousand. Let's just close it."

"He needs to resign," I say, but I alt-tab over to the spreadsheet, to see if her proposal is within the realm of possibility, and then it catches up with me—she's just told me he's guilty.

"Come on, he's forty-five," Beth says. "What's he supposed to do?"

"That's really not my problem. He doesn't belong in a classroom."

"Is that what the investigator found? I don't think so." She's right: all the investigator really turned up were a few witnesses who saw him with the girl outside of school—no hotel rooms, no text messages.

I scan the spreadsheet of other settlements for one that might have been anything like this one—I filter for Severity of Offense (three) and Strength of our Case (one).

"He walks away now and we give him thirty thousand dollars in lieu of his pension," I offer.

"That's laughable, Nora."

"That's my offer."

"I'll take it to him, but I'm not optimistic," she says.

"Good."

"I'm sorry if I was brusque—I just want to get this out of the way, okay?"

"Me, too."

"And then we'll talk. Promise?"

"Okay," I say.

But is it? Was Beth also on that Facebook thread, under some assumed name? It's still open on my computer and I scan it again. Is she the one who went to visit him in Vermont and obtained an apology? The one half-defending him for teaching us to think critically, to Question Authority? (He wore that button all the time but I misinterpreted its meaning: that "question" was a verb never even occurred to me. I thought he'd dubbed himself the authority on all questions.) She could even have been Patty Hearst, the one who got pregnant and who still hears his voice in her head.

14

Naomi

There's a saying that only the dead know Brooklyn. It's also true of Facebook. You don't know what haunting is until you've felt yourself sucked through the pneumatic tubes of that place—so many spirits summoned, so much unrest and churning. If I believed in such things, I'd say it was purgatory. That said, I find this particular tangle, the stories about Bob, to be the worst of the worst. I say "stories" like my ma used to: to mean anyone's way of getting another person to listen. I am wrapped up in all those stories like a fly in a spiderweb.

Nora was a tough one, or had a tough mouth. He called her "Trouble," but not to her face. When she didn't come with us out west, I was glad for her, relieved. I'd gone from fearing her as brave enough to expose him, to worrying she'd become his particular dragon to slay, to wishing her safe and free. Not that I discussed these thoughts—my only confidant was my husband and our only secrets were his secrets. "Trouble" was not one of his better efforts—he needed to get to know her better so he could hit on the right one and that never happened. Carnal knowledge was not always enough. (Once upon a time I was only "Cousin Jane"—wasn't till after a year of marriage he hit on "Juanita.") Still, their session in the darkroom should have done the trick. I'd have called her "Persephone" for visiting the underworld and getting out. He told me all of it: that he'd "sampled the merchandise" and that "the merchandise had objected." Well, they couldn't all fall over so easily, now could they? Nora's snub rolled off him like water off a duck, of course—it was only me that feared she'd say something, call someone. She seemed different.

But not one of them ever dropped the dime on him, not while they could still have a claim. Why not? Was the sisterhood that powerful? Even after we sent them home from Arizona, no one got the whole story. At least not out of any of the girls. They fell in with each other, refused to break ranks. And we wanted to get out of New York anyway, so that agreement with the Academy wasn't hard to sign. Paranoia was the tune of the times then, even for us—the drug-free, all-natural, silly hippies of Willow Street.

I thought I was happy all those years, but I never had so much freedom as Nora, who said no.

15
Nora

To my amazement, Ktanya has come around the bend to my cube entrance and is looking at me with what appears to be concern. Did I raise my voice on the phone with Beth? Have I been talking to myself?

"What's going on?"

"Jocelyn gave me this case—the hearing's on Monday."

"And?"

"The guy's a pedophile."

"That's for definite?"

"Sort of. I mean no one's ever caught him at it—they just gave him a bunch of Unsatisfactories and fined him but I can tell he's not right. Still, our paper trail sucks. I just offered him thirty thousand bucks to stop teaching and I really don't know if I can go up—it makes me too sick."

Ktanya gives me a "Really?" look. I notice that her manicure matches her belt, red and black.

"You can't take it personally."

"But couldn't I just let it go to hearing? Maybe we'll win."

She shakes her head but I can tell she's also sympathetic. "Didn't I hear Gina Alessandro offer to help you earlier?"

Of course I know that Ktanya can hear everything in my cube but I'm kind of surprised that she listens.

"C'mon," she says.

So I follow her down the cubicle alleys to Gina's cube, across the floor. It's twice the size of my own, with higher walls, and more snapshots than anyone else's that I've ever seen. Many of them appear to involve parties. Gina is simultaneously putting on her coat, sorting paperwork into her briefcase, and talking on the phone. Ktanya raps symbolically on the soft cubicle wall and Gina looks up at her, then smiles a genuine, brilliant smile. She mimes "one second," and then "blah-blah-blah," and then says out loud into the phone, "Look, I've gotta go. I've got a hearing in half an hour. Talk to you later, okay?" and hangs up.

"What's up?" she says, in a way that makes it sound like we're all going out for beers.

Ktanya says, "I think Nora was feeling shy."

Embarrassed, I jump in: "I see you're on your way out the door, I just—you said to ask you for help any time."

Gina nods. "Tell me."

"I want to let it go to hearing."

"What's that going to accomplish, if you've got no case?"

"I just talked to opposing counsel and she doubled her offer in like five minutes."

Gina nods, acknowledging that this means something. "But you have an offer out. Are you saying you're going to rescind it?"

Then there's a silence, in which I realize that's what I'm saying, and how far outside normal procedure that would be, and that what I'm really asking is for her to take the case herself, because I can already tell she likes to swim against the tide.

"I'm booked solid with appeals," she says, as her eyes scan the surrounding cubicles, taking inventory. "Listen, ask Jessica. She owes me one. Tell her I'm calling it in. And it's not like she's never argued a case with no evidence before—I've seen her do it."

"Who's Jessica?"

"The tall one. Third cube down."

We find Jessica regarding five piles of overfull manila folders with great intensity. She is indeed tall, and very pale, and she looks a little bit like a prairie dog. Maybe it's just because of the way she is standing in her cube, with her hands dangling and her neck long. Ktanya has said her name twice when I see that Jessica has headphones on so I tap her, gently, and she jumps about a foot, pulling at her earbuds as though they have attacked her.

"Hi," I say, "Gina said you could help us. She said . . ."

"Slow down, Tiger," whispers Ktanya, but not before I've said, "She says you owe her one."

Jessica wrinkles her forehead. "I thought she'd forgotten that."

"We need someone to take this case to hearing Monday morning. It's a pervert teacher," says Ktanya. I love the way she has taken this on—I want to hug her.

"Can we prove it?" Without waiting for an answer, she then asks, "Who's opposing?"

"Beth—Elizabeth Cohen. At Rachman Weeks."

She shakes her head. "Don't know her." She is very subtly bouncing her weight from one foot to the other as she stands there. I wonder if she is addicted to exercise. I've heard that's a thing.

"Any witnesses, at all?"

"Not in this one."

"There's another one?"

"Five years ago, decided in his favor."

"Get me one of them, then."

"But we lost."

"They might see things differently now. Right?"

I nod. She keeps talking: "I don't have time to do the foot-work but if you can find me a girl who's willing to go on re-cord, I'll do it."

"And if I can't?"

She shakes her head. "I can't afford another loss this quar-ter. I need my job, you know?"

I know. So does Ktanya. I look at my watch: it's 3:20.

I go back to my desk and open up the folder for the earlier case. Beth was not representing him then—he had a regular teacher's union attorney. There are at least a hundred pages of transcripts in the folder and the idea of reading through them is overwhelming. Even in a good case, transcripts are nothing like what's in movies and TV. Most of the time the witnesses are just establishing that people really are who they say they are, or were where they said they were, and the important points never seem to catch my eye on a first pass. People say so much that isn't relevant. I've already scanned this stuff once, but I didn't take any notes because I was in a hurry, and so I can't remember the girl's name. All I can retrieve is the name of her school, Hilda Conkling, because Hilda Conkling was a correspondent of my grandfather's—she was an eight- or nine-year-old poetess, briefly famous in the early twenties. Then she disappeared, or, as I found out one afternoon on the internet, turned into a reference librarian at Smith College where she lived in happy obscurity until her death. My grandfather, the famous poet, admired her "modernist tendencies," although I suspect he also had a creepy old-man crush on her.

I sort through the other contents of the file: evaluations, letters from the principal, photocopies of time cards—and a stapled booklet. I'd assumed it was an employee handbook or something on my first pass, but now that I've got it in front of me I see it's one of those compendiums of student writing that was (or maybe still is) the centerpiece of a certain approach to teaching middle school kids the mechanics of draft-revise-publish. On the cover is the title: "Can I Get a Witness?" and I notice that what looks at first like a drop shadow behind the "I" is actually a hieroglyphic representation of the twin towers—the booklet is from the 2001–2002 school year. These kids were like five blocks away from the Trade Center. They must have thought the world had ended. I thumb through the publication, scanning the names of the kids and the titles of their works. I do not read the prose piece titled "Lost Dogs of 9/11," and also avoid the item titled "Lies from the EPA" because I don't really want to know what's in my epithelium. Then I get to a page that has the imprint of a ghostly paperclip and I realize this is why the thing is in the file, this is the evidence. It's a poem—it's called "You Told Me, You Said":

Fourteen is old enough
You told me
You meant, to have an opinion,
Or maybe, to ride the subway alone.

You told me I saw clearly.
You told me my eyes were gold.
I collected the bits,
Burnt papers, lost letters
That scattered.
They just made me sadder.
Fourteen is old enough, you said.

I was producing the same palaver at that age—pages of it, though I never showed it to anyone. I was ashamed of my poetry the same way I was ashamed of my wrong-brand jeans, the apartment we lived in, my mother's job (everyone knows psychologists' kids are totally fucked up), my missing father, even my name: Eleanor. Did I say "fucked up" yet? Probably not. The poem in the Singer file is by a girl named Elodie Cascarelli. What a name; maybe her eyes *were* gold. Or maybe he meant her ability to see was a treasure. Or maybe he never said any of it. At Music & Art, I knew a girl who was always publishing poems in the literary magazine that made it sound like she was living in a Henry Miller novel but she was mousy and shy and had never even been on a date.

In eighth grade, our book of class writings was called the *Tis Bottle*. When handing out the new pages each week, Rasmussen liked to falsetto the refrain from Aretha's "Rock Steady" with a downbeat emphasis that turned "what it is" into "what it TIS!" My mental picture of this still amuses me: a six-foot-four-inch red-haired man in a Mexican poncho, rolling his gait like a black dude—it never failed to make us giggle and love him. Even those of us who didn't really love him at all.

Our class book was named after the following joke:

There was a man who spent his whole life searching for the Tis Bottle. He travels the seven continents and the seven seas. After thirty years, he finds himself at a temple in the Himalayas, where he is finally granted an audience with the head swami, the top lama. "Do you have it? Can I see it?" the man begs, even though he's starving, hasn't slept in weeks, and is nearly a hundred years old at this point. The holy man beckons him into a cave-like room completely filled with soda bottles—all different colors, brands, sizes, some full, some half-full, some empty. The sage blows gently across the rim of one of the bottles to sound a note, shuffles over to another and does the same to produce a new note, and on to a third. He offers the fourth bottle to the visitor, who cradles it in his hands, blows tremulously over its aperture, and promptly dies of happiness. The note he has produced corresponds to the third word in the sung phrase, "My Country 'Tis of Thee."

He had a different joke every year, which provided a different you-had-to-be-in-on-it name for the class publication— *Mel Famey* (he walks a batter after drinking a beer: the beer that made Mel Famey walk us), *Moogli!* (a guy who thinks he's avoided cannibalism and sexual assault by performing some heinous act, only to hear the headhunter chieftain announce, "Now, Moogli!"), and so on. There was no close textual analysis of the content—they were really all one joke, anyway, the lesson of which was "never assume anything," which was the scaffold of Bob's teaching philosophy. If he taught us nothing else, he taught us to doubt, to call bullshit.

I google "Elodie Cascarelli." I find that for a while she kept a blog about urban beekeeping, BeeLoudGlade, but the last entry is two years old. I find ten Cascarellis with New York phone numbers, but not one of them answers the phone, and of the three with human voices on their outgoing messages, two are male and one is a woman with what sounds like a Russian accent. I leave voicemails with my office phone number on the first three; on the other two I include my cell number as well, because it's really time to leave if I'm going to get my cat back.

Facebook has been sitting open in my browser this whole time and I finally realize I can look for Elodie there, and voila: she is a thin and oddly beautiful young woman with Pre-Raphaelite hair. She went to Oberlin. She likes The White Stripes. The most recent thing on her page is a beautiful picture of Elodie at a younger age, maybe nine or ten, with extremely short hair and freckles, apparently perched in a tree. It was posted February 15, 2005. Underneath it are comments:

> **Zadie Collins** *Goodbye, dear Elodie. This is how I will always remember you.*
> **Meredith Catniss** *Don't say that, she's not gone!*
> **Zadie Collins** *I'll never see her again. I'm allowed to mourn.*
> **Meredith Catniss** *You will never see her, but you will see him!*
> **Zadie Collins** *Obv*

I puzzle over this for a bit, and conclude that Elodie is dead. I consider that she is just leaving the country or something, but her friend's certainty that she'll never be seen again weighs against that theory. I rustle around in my cache of papers until I find the hearing decision from her case against Singer, in which he was fined and suspended but not fired. Elodie didn't testify. The decision was issued February 10, 2005. Did she kill herself because of this? Is Singer the "him" her friend mentions?

Under my own name, I leave a comment on her wall: *I am investigating a teacher in the public school system regarding an open case. If any of Elodie's friends would be willing to talk to me about this, please call me.* I leave my work number.

I try to imagine how I would have reacted to losing a friend to suicide at that age—claiming my need to mourn in a public place would certainly not have been my style. It still isn't. Anyway, if Elodie is dead, this is officially a blind alley. I am going to get my cat.

16
Nora

I t feels good to be outside. I walk to Cadman Plaza by the post office, a landmark of my childhood, and decide I will cut through the park. Waiting for the light at Tillary Street, I find myself looking across the newly AstroTurfed playing field and remember how, in ninth grade, Beth and I used to smoke pot (me) and meet boys (her) behind the war monument. It always wound up with me making awkward conversation with the sidekick while she went off in the bushes to fool around with Tyrone or Sadiq. I can see myself and the other guy, sitting on the edge of the monument, chucking rocks at squirrels and pigeons while attempting to make conversation about our somewhat limited shared culture. No eye contact; we talked while facing outward. I did learn, from one of them, to distinguish between various types of ghetto headgear—Kangol, applejack, tam—and even how a dry cleaning bag was used to puff out the crown of the latter two items so as to balance out the afro underneath. I liked the idea of the tough kids I saw on the subway, primping their hats to get the look just right. I guess I also picked up some other useful knowledge during those sessions—what music was important at the moment, proper slang locutions, sneaker taxonomy . . . and how to give off some mysterious vibe that ensured no man ever made the first move on me—even when I wanted him to.

There's still grimy snow at the curb and the wind cuts right through me as I walk parallel to the towers of Cadman Plaza through the alley of bare London planetrees in the park. When I was young, this area was going to be a shining city of affordable housing and common spaces—and for years it seemed as though any time I entered the north end of the Heights, I was under a construction bridge or avoiding a gantlet of hard-hatted men of the sort who attacked anti-war protesters. We would be playing Ringolevio or Sardines but then the perfect hiding place would turn out to be the claimed domain of some towering dude in rags, or a trysting place for un-fun-looking sex, or a public urinal. All along Clinton, Clark, and Fulton Streets the vacant lots were enclosed in a picket of old tenement doors, their interior paint faded to the colors of Necco Wafers. I have a weird nostalgia for those doors. They remind me of the saying, "safe as houses." Of course, I've never lived in a house. The only person I knew who lived in a house was Beth—a huge house in Kensington, with plastic slipcovers on the "good" furniture and sugar-free candy in a dish by the front door.

Walking down Middagh Street I wonder if Cat Rescuer Guy is a bit sketchy—this end of the neighborhood still feels a little hostile to me. When I was a kid, it was deserted around here; kids even played stickball in the street. The occasional car came through at a crawl, trolling for parking, and people thought it was safe until a kid got hit running for a ball and never recovered.

At the corner of Poplar and Henry, I scan the block ahead, trying to discern my destination. There's one apartment building mid-block that I have a mental picture of—it always seems to have people's used clothing and books piled up outside. I have assumed it to be my destination today—where I mentally placed Cat Guy when he said "Poplar Street." Now I'm feeling uneasy about this mission. I don't like strangers, strange men in particular, and now what am I doing? Going to meet one, alone. I think as hard as I can of Tin Man's silver paw, the way it felt when he extended his claws just a little, as though responding to my hand-holding the way a human might.

It turns out Everett, as he introduces himself, lives in the fancy new condo building on the corner. It's still got the sign up, advertising available units. So he's not a character from a Tom Waits song but some millionaire who rescues cats and works nights. His fourth-floor apartment is practically a loft—I can't even smell the multiple cats that live there with him and his girlfriend or wife. (There is a strangely evocative array of women's shoes lined up near the door: a huge relief.) I follow him through his dramatically sun-dappled and cat-infested living-dining-kitchen space to the bathroom where the latest rescue is cloistered.

"Here, this is the guy," he says, opening the door to reveal a skinny, miserable creature much more tabby than tiger. He mews at us dolefully.

"Not mine," I say and my chest collapses.

"Do you want him? You could foster him . . ."

"No, thanks. I guess I'm a one-cat household."

"Right," Everett says, as though I've said I believe in slavery.

"Mine's grayer than that, and bigger, and not as skinny . . . if you see him."

"No collar?"

"He has a collar."

"You let him out? In the city?"

"I don't have a 'country,'" I say, defensively. "Anyway, if you see him . . ." I turn and walk back across his living room, heading for the door, determined not to weep. He walks ahead of me toward the entrance. In his wake, cats look up and resettle in their various sleeping spots.

"Good luck finding him," he says, as he opens his apartment door and skillfully blocks the attempted exit of a small black thing with his foot.

I adopted Tin Man at some cat rescuer jamboree at the Union Square Petco and I signed a contract saying I'd follow all their rules (shots, regular vet visits, *indoors only*). But the deal I made with myself was different: I would provide food, water, a place to shit, and a place to sleep. I would admire him from a distance as he slept on a sunny windowsill and scratch behind his ears if he deposited himself on my lap. But my cat bolted out the apartment door every time I opened it. So I took him down to the laundry room a few times and then one summer night I opened the service entrance to see what he would do. And that first time, he glanced at me before walking away; the second time, not. "He's a cat," I told myself, which meant that I respected his autonomy and that he is only an animal, and that I should know better than to get too attached.

I have been walking down Willow Street at a brisk pace and my nose is running. I stop and fish around in my bag for a tissue. I am essentially across the street from the ornate terracotta façade of the old Academy building, now condos. The eighth-grade classroom was on the third floor and my seat was beside the northernmost window. I would gaze out at Rasmussen's brownstone near the next corner, with its ridiculous red-and-black-and-green-painted stoop, and wonder why I felt so left out. It wasn't just Beth who'd fallen under his spell—there were about six of them, coming and going like his brownstone was some kind of clubhouse, hanging around after school when they were supposed to be over at the Heights Casino, playing tennis; or at the Roosa School of Music, studying piano and violin.

My big project that year was a "report" (as we called those things that were not essays or reviews or any other now-familiar form of prose expression) on the teachers' strike of 1969. It's difficult to imagine what *research* then meant to me, or how I went about identifying sources, but Rasmussen offered me his "archives" at home as a resource. I was fourteen but I was still secretly searching for a secret passageway or a false-fronted fireplace, some entrance to Narnia, and I accepted his offer as much because I wanted to explore his house as for any other reason. His study was on the second floor, above the living room. It did contain a fireplace and the fireplace did have decorative grillwork and some kind of iridescent glazing on its tiles, but it was not a portal to another dimension and otherwise the study was just a book-lined room with a lumpy green couch in it—nowhere near as cool as the library in my grandfather's apartment. I sat there for about an hour, reading back issues of *Ramparts* and the *New Yorker* and taking notes.

When I crossed the hall to use the bathroom, I glanced into the master bedroom, which contained an immense waterbed under a canopy made by a purple tie-dyed sheet. The canopy matched the color of the stained-glass window lozenges almost perfectly. I didn't sit down on the waterbed, but I was standing in front of it, wonderingly, when Tamsin Green padded into the room, wearing nothing but a T-shirt and underpants. Tamsin was a year older than me—attending high school at that point. I knew her by sight, but I had never actually spoken to her. I knew she was especially close to Rasmussen because I had noticed them joking around together at school the year before. I also knew that her parents were divorced and that she was, like me, effectively fatherless. We were supposed to know and like each other because of this in the eyes of one or more adults at school, but there has never been a worse reason for liking someone, if you ask me, than that you share a common flaw. She saw me standing stupidly in front of Bob and Naomi's bed and said "Hi," before seating herself carefully and skillfully on the rolling seas. I then realized that she had been resting there before I came in: there was a box of Kleenex on the bedside table next to a splayed-open copy of *Demian* by Hermann Hesse. She picked up the book, and I said "Hi," back and then scooted back to the study, hoping she wouldn't tell on me for snooping.

17
Nora

Tamsin is the one in that photograph that sometimes haunts me, with her ribcage crosshatched by shadows. I was under the impression that her divorced parents were media big shots—screenwriters or something. She sometimes flew to the Hamptons for the weekend. And I'd heard that they were the ones who extracted Rasmussen's agreement to stay out of New York for ten years after the arrest in Arizona. There was no sex offender registry back then. Still, it seemed an arbitrary and limited boundary. Tamsin had been famously inconsolable.

She looked me up once, in 1995 or so, when we were all new and enthusiastic email users. Her message came under the subject line "worms!" which referred to a lunchtime ritual at the Academy. It consisted of someone tricking someone else into saying the word "worms," which was the signal for everyone else to throw the contents of their water glasses at the victim. The amazing thing about this game is that it worked more than once. Conversations about fishing, gardening, and internal parasites were all equally rare in our cohort and should have caused immediate suspicion. But Rasmussen had the God-given ability to start a fight on any subject, and that was the trick. He'd get you off on some tangent where you were defending what you knew to be true (fish don't have legs, normal body temperature is 98.6°) so vehemently that you wouldn't notice as you'd turned the corner into dangerous territory. The moment the word left your mouth you knew it, though, so there was a horrible freezeframe of inevitability, self-recrimination, and physical stress before the cannonade let loose.

I hadn't thought about "worms" for thirty years and, seeing the word, and Tamsin's name, I was just flattered to be remembered and curious as to why, of all people, she would look me up. Her note was brief: "This is a voice from your past! I'm so glad I found you!" and the explanation that she was in from her new home in Tucson because her grandmother was ill. We made plans over email to meet at the Odeon, one of the few places in New York City we both knew from what even white girls like us had begun to call "back in the day." When she came up to me, I was sitting at the bar and she said, "Hello, stranger," and I just stared. For one thing, she was alarmingly thin, but also her face had changed. It was as though her features had been shaken up and reassembled, thrown like a handful of jacks.

"My face," she said. "I was in a car crash—I lost my looks."

"I'm so sorry!" I said, which sounded like I was agreeing with her last remark though I wasn't. She looked no less pretty, except insofar as any forty-year-old woman looks less pretty than any teenager and any anorexic begins to look a little like her own corpse. She must have been used to people saying sorry, though.

"I'm fine. Just a little Humpty Dumpty action—check it out." And then I did know her, because "check it out" had been so much a part of her speech, our speech, back then. She had a husky, sexy voice that had been way out of place in her underdeveloped body of once upon a time. I got off my barstool and hugged her.

We found a table and fortunately—or unfortunately—ordered martinis. It was fortunate because, drunk, it all seemed funny and long ago, but unfortunate because I soon saw that more than Tamsin's face was broken. Her story was simple, more or less. The car accident—a head-on collision at a stop sign—had ended her college education and financed the next ten years of her life. The other driver's insurance had paid her medical bills and a hundred thousand dollars in damages. In retrospect, she said, she should have asked for much more. Her chances of ever becoming a model had been ruined, and she could have been, she insisted. I didn't disagree. Also, her short-term memory had been affected, she couldn't really grip with her left hand, and she only had one working lung. She had spent all the money, however, by the time she was twenty-eight. "I bought a huge television," she told me, "and a lot of dinners in nice restaurants." The rich parents were, it seemed, no longer rich or, in any case, no longer in the picture.

Over dinner, she mentioned Rasmussen—in an aside, but as though he were a current and relevant point of reference. I asked her if she still thought about him a lot.

"I'm so sick of that story," she said. "I used to think it defined me, you know?" She flipped her hair over her ear with a characteristic motion, a small gesture that drew attention to the silver bracelet on her wrist. Then I realized that she was dressed almost exactly the way we all used to dress at the Academy: Levi's, smock-y shirt from India, cowboy boots. She saw my eye on the bracelet and put her hand in her lap.

It was almost identical to the one Naomi used to wear, and the one Beth had had, and there were others—engraved with secret messages from Bob (or so Beth had always implied), but I saw hers once and I'm pretty sure it was just his special name for her. They all had nicknames: Uhura, Tiddlywinks, Sloopy. Tamsin's was Christmas.

"I was in love with him," she said then.

"I guess we all were, a little," I said, though I was surprised to hear myself say it.

"Not like that." She shook her head and I saw that her eyes were wet. "Really in love. I thought we were going to grow old together."

"But he raped you," I said, ignoring her feelings in the hope that she would do likewise—I really didn't want to be sitting at the Odeon with a weeping hippie skeleton.

"Who told you that?"

"No one told me. I mean, I know you thought you were willing but you were just a kid."

"I tried to say no but it happened anyway. With Naomi lying there next to me, holding my hand."

"Jesus. Really?"

Tamsin nodded, with a quizzical expression as if to say, *I know, crazy, right?* "It was a Sunday morning. He made waffles."

"You said you were in love with him."

"I was. I thought I was. I don't know. At that moment I was scared to death but then I couldn't un-happen it, right? A week later I wanted to move into their house."

I had been envious of Tamsin when we were at the Academy. She was gentle, and frail, and ethereally beautiful. We all wore our hair the same way then: long and center-parted. But Tamsin's looked the most like Naomi's—thick enough to make a true curtain over one eye, as it does in that photo of her naked, at fourteen. She looked like she belonged to both of them, a daughter and a sister at the same time.

After dinner, Tamsin and I took a walk across the Brooklyn Bridge. It was a clear fall day and the walkway was dense with tourists. At the second tower, we stopped with the rest of them to look out across the harbor and Tamsin returned to the subject of Rasmussen. "Naomi wasn't his first wife, you know. There was Lee Ann. They got together at boarding school. They were just kids."

"So what happened to her?" I asked.

"They ran away together—hopped freight trains. Her parents were outraged and kept them apart. I think she killed herself."

"It sounds like an opera or something." I meant that I didn't believe a word—the story was too close to the one I'd heard about Tamsin, herself—the parental fortress, the agonized girl. At least she hadn't killed herself.

"It was heavy for him," she went on. "He never got over her."

"And she never got over him," I said, almost reflexively. I detested stories of young love gone wrong, always had. "So why'd you look me up, anyway?" I asked her—in part to cover my reaction.

"Well, to be honest, I thought you could help me out," she said.

At the time, I was working as a freelance copyeditor and living in an East Village walk-up with the bathtub in the kitchen. I had no assets to speak of but I knew the "help" she had in mind was financial; she'd been setting it up all evening.

"Wow, Tamsin. I'm totally broke, I'm sorry."

"But—your grandfather. I mean, he was on a stamp."

"Yeah, well, if he left anything behind, my mother's got it."

She believed me, I could tell—it was the truth.

"I just thought . . . even if it was like a job or something to come back to. I'm done with Tucson."

"You can stay in my apartment for a week, if that helps, but I warn you there's no couch and the roaches have not entirely checked out."

We emailed a few times after that, and spoke on the phone once. In that conversation, I asked her why she didn't ask Rasmussen for help (she'd given me the impression they were still in touch).

"I did go looking for him, actually," she said. "To his parents' summer place in Vermont. I knew that's where he'd be. It was right after my accident."

"And?"

"He apologized."

I couldn't picture this.

"He said he thought he was rescuing me back then. From my crazy parents. You have no idea how crazy they were."

"The only person he was taking care of was himself," I blurted.

"He never really messed with you, did he?" she said. It was a non sequitur, but also a jab.

"Not really," I said.

"I guess you're still jealous," she said then.

"Go fuck yourself," I told her, or words to that effect.

Of course, she had a point. I did feel left out of their little cult. Even back in 1990-whenever-that-was when Tamsin showed up, I still felt it. It's amazing how long these things take to get sorted out.

18

Naomi

I grew up in a two-room house in Sherrard, West Virginia. Front room, back room. We slept in the back—me, my folks, my two sisters, my brother, Duff. When I left them all behind was the first time I thought of myself as a sinner. Because even though I taught myself to sleep through the night, to sleep through anything at all, I knew I was leaving my sisters in the hands of the devil. We weren't churchgoing so I'm not being biblical: my daddy was just a man of no conscience and no love in his heart. Bob has many flaws but there's no comparison. I can promise you that he feels what happened to our family like a stake in his heart. I know that.

About his students, Bob had more of a blind spot. He believed he was helping them grow up, teaching them . . . he was gentle. "Foreplay" sounds wrong—always has—but there were preliminaries, opening acts. That sounds wrong, too. I just know the only tears I ever saw were jealous ones or from normal injuries—anger, loss.

Yet then there's a story like Tamsin's. I don't remember holding her hand, but I believe her. There must be so much I don't dare remember, even now. You think of your young self as being just like your grown one—I do. But there must have been a time in my life where I was two people, or four, or eight: enough versions of me to thin out the horror, enough different pairs of eyes and ears that it was possible to bear witness from a distance, even right there in the same bed.

19
Nora

I backtrack to Hicks Street to say hello to Sami at the pet store and thank him for sending Everett to me. He's not at the front counter—it's too cold to sit down there by the door—but he's up in the loft where his television is, watching the news. He recognizes me and greets me: "Nora! How *are* you?" He starts down the stairs.

"You don't have to come down," I say.

"For you? Anything is possible." He's such a flirt but would obviously never overstep by even an inch. At least, I believe this about him—he fasts during Ramadan. He comes downstairs anyway.

"I just wanted to thank you for spreading the word to Everett."

"Everett?"

"The cat rescuer? Little guy with freckles?"

"Sure, that guy. Of course. He found Tin Man?" His already generous forehead softens further, anticipating the joy and relief of my reunion with my lost cat. I hate to disappoint him.

"No, false alarm. But it gave me hope. Maybe someone has him. I'd decided he was dead. It's been so cold . . ."

"No, no. Don't give up hope. Tin Man will return to you! Or I'll find you a nice kitten!"

I laugh. "You just hate to lose a customer," I joke.

"Every customer counts," says Sami.

"Well, thanks again," I say, as the door opens and a woman with an immense blond dog enters to replace me. The dog sits obediently in front of the counter and Sami provides it with a treat without taking his eyes off its owner, with whom he is already fully engaged.

Outside the pet store, I turn right and walk into the west wind. This last block is the hardest part of my day sometimes—after the commercial part of Montague Street ends, and there is no reason for me to keep walking except to get home, even though it is not yet six o'clock. My apartment is essentially empty as well as haunted. The building is just past the entrance to the Promenade—it's like a vast ship of red brick and white cornices, moored at the edge of New York Harbor: the "best address" in Brooklyn Heights according to some, although as a child I always thought it would be better to live in a brownstone. I assumed such a home automatically included a more conventional family than the isosceles triangles I lived in: Adeline, me, and my grandfather; or later, briefly, my stepfather; or later still, our Siamese cat, Anna, named for Freud's daughter. God help us all. My mother's practice was on the ground floor. I have known José, the head doorman, and Victor, the super, for longer than I've known anyone else in the city, or the world. They are unfailingly nice to me still, which is another thing I hate about coming home now that I live here again. José is on duty most evenings, and he greets me so warmly, and I am grateful but I have no small talk in me. I never have.

I smile and say hello as brightly as I know how, and I ask him how he is and look him in the eye when he gives a pro forma answer, but the follow-up questions about family and vacations and everything else are just beyond me.

"Still no cat?" he offers.

I shake my head.

"I look for him every night, by the dryers, after my shift. I keep an eye out." He nods as he says this. He must be almost seventy by now, but his hair is black and shiny and beautifully combed. Sometimes I wonder if he is gay—if working here, in this neighborhood, gave him a bigger life than was available for a Cuban-American guy in Queens in 1970, or whenever he first put on that green-and-gold-piped uniform. It could be the last job in America that still requires a costume.

"Thanks, José," I say. I am waiting for the day when I add, "Don't bother," or "It's okay," but that day hasn't arrived yet.

The first thing I see when the elevator door opens into my apartment is the telephone nook, a wood-paneled alcove with a built-in secretarial table, kind of like an old-fashioned phone booth but bigger. If I were going to take a photograph that represented the peculiar blend of luxury and exhaustion that characterizes this apartment, it would be of this strange piece of furniture, struck by late-afternoon light. The phone is a block of olive-green plastic with a rotary dial. In the center of the dial is a disk that tells us the number, which begins with the word "ULster." Most of the people who had that number memorized are probably dead. On the floor underneath the phone, garlanded in its grimy spiral cord, is an answering machine—perhaps the last of its kind. The outgoing message has my mother's voice on it so I can't throw it out.

I thought she'd never leave, is the truth of it, because when I was a kid, she never could. We'd get to the door and go nowhere. Then she would unpack her purse: lipstick, tissues, Belairs, matches, paperback, checkbook, address book, perfume atomizer—good God, what else? It was like a magic trick, the bottomless handbag. "Keys, where are my goddamned keys?" She kept them on a sandwich-bag twist tie. I have barely cried since her death, hardly even spoken her name. Sometimes I think that's because I had Tin Man, who used to greet me at the door, who stopped me from falling into fugue states like this one.

With my coat still on, I wander down the hallway to the library and turn on the stupid floor lamp I had to get to replace the Tiffany sconces that I sold, along with my grandfather's collection of first editions, and the oriental rugs, and the Stickley chairs and the Spode and the side tables and everything else that paid for my mother's last folly: dying with no will. My grandfather, Virgil Falsington, was a poet made famous by the success of just one poem, an artifact of its time called "The Pursuit of Virtue at Brooklyn Heights." No one's ever heard of it now, except the occasional scholar, even though it's in every American poetry anthology published before about 1950. This apartment, the "poet's mansion in the sky," was crucial to the prestige of the building when they first opened it for rental in 1922—I've seen the old ads on the internet.

Sometimes I wonder if, born fifty years later, Granddad would have been a rock star. He had the flamboyant affect and enormous self-regard—and his big hit turned out to be an eyelash in the fossil record of American self-definition, comparable to, say, "Build Me Up Buttercup," or, perhaps more fairly, a lesser Bob Dylan ballad—it was topical but ultimately insipid. In it, he represented the principle of virtue as a girl-child in a nightgown, awakened from a bad dream. At least, I think that's what she represents, otherwise I have no idea what the title refers to. When he wrote it, they were still working on the first draft of the great American archetypes: cowboy, vamp, gangster, robber baron, gentleman explorer . . . "The Pursuit of Virtue" doesn't seem to be about America, but it has to be, on some level; how else could it have been both so successful and so ephemeral? It rhymed like a motherfucking sewing machine and still I couldn't memorize it. Because it was my legacy, I guess.

The library was always my favorite room—with its Greek key cornices and rolling stepladder—a temple of learning, et cetera, but now it just looks like a ruin. What's left are the books no one wants: the collected works of Granddad; well-toasted Harper Colophons from my mother's college days— Erich Fromm, Rollo May—and, behind the door, my own special hutch of childhood favorites: Oz, Kipling, *Harriet the Spy*, *Cress Delahanty*, the Lang fairy tale collections bound in colored cloth. On the shelf above these, the top shelf, are my journals, notebooks, and other paper keepsakes, including the *Tis Bottle*, which I unshelve and carry back to the windowsill and to the lamplight. I haven't opened it in twenty years, maybe more.

The pasteboard covers of the binder are velvety and almost colorless, though inside I can see that they were formerly blue. The prongs of the ACCO fastener have rusted where the tiny sliders have been holding them, and the lavender mimeo ink is so faint it's almost invisible. The title page, like everything else in the volume, is hand-lettered by Naomi Rasmussen: the sight of her handwriting, with its typewriter-style lowercase *a*'s and *g*'s, twangs some inner guitar for me. I must have spent hours trying to imitate that clear, even hand.

Tucked among the first few pages I find a folded piece of purple stationery: a letter I wrote to Beth on July 10, 1973, and apparently never sent.

Dear Beth,

I am still mad at you and I don't think it has anything to do with my "competitive streak" or that I need to be right all the time. What if I am legitimately worried about you? I can't believe you forgot everything we said. I'm not saying he's going to take you into white slavery but the point is he actually could. Some of those states out west, you can like marry a girl at 12. And also prostitution is legal. Remember how he said there was no such thing as rape because the girl has to want it for it to work? He lied. You should read the article in Ramparts. *So I didn't "chicken out," I made a smart decision. I bet someday you'll agree with me, too.*

My summer is going OK. Camp is not as fun this year because everyone is "going steady" or spending a ridiculous amount of time walking around with their hands in each other's pockets, etc., which makes me a little sick because it reminds me so much of you-know-who. Except the boys my age are such unmitigated morons I can't believe my friends can even tolerate them for five minutes. I always wish I went to school with boys until I get to camp and remember what they're like.

I have a crush on a counselor named Adam. He gave me this amazing book called The Dharma Bums *and it's changing my whole way of thinking. There are so many things Rasmussen never even talks about. All he knows is politics and folk music and oppressed black people. I wish I could write like this Kerouac guy does. It's all in a rush but it makes sense in a different way. Tumbles of mad-poet meaning like crazy rivers full of genius Buddhas swimming with salmon upstream. (I am mixing it up with the trying to write like Holden Caulfield, I think.)*

The letter ends there. I guess I was embarrassed by my attempt to write like Kerouac, which Beth would never have gotten, anyway. I tried to write like Holden Caulfield in my journal once, and Rasmussen scribbled in the margin with his red pen, "Nice try, Phoebe!" I was half-humiliated by my own need for approval but also half-exalted—because the reference to Holden's kid sister indicated that he'd seen what I was trying to do. But no one was going to "get" my Kerouac riff, except maybe that cute counselor, who kissed me on the lips at the end of that summer. No tongue, but it was still my first real kiss, and time cooperatively slowed down enough that I was able to record and later replay the moment for myself many times—the softness of his lips as well as my realization that I must have actually meant something to him, that he wanted to kiss me. We had only talked a few times before dinner and once after he had put his campers (the littlest boys) to bed. Mostly, I'd admired him from a distance, memorizing his helpless-looking eyes when he took off his thick eyeglasses, his funny way of ushering his kids around with his hands fully spread like starfish, flapping at the wrists. In his tattered madras shirt, open on a hot day, he had the chest of a boy.

I turn the brittle pages of the *Tis Bottle* carefully until I see Beth's name under the heading "My Son, the Doctor."

Harvey, Harvey, my son, my son
Listen while I kvell
My boy, you will outshine the sun
Your pop can go to hell.

You are my bar mitzvah boy
Today, you are a man.
You'll be as good as anyone
A doctor, like we planned.

No schmatta trade for you, my peach
Nothing but the best.
We'll move down to Miami Beach
When your father's laid to rest.

I don't remember Beth being witty. I don't remember her trading in Yiddishisms, either. She must have been listening to Alan Sherman records. I was always certain that I was smarter than she was—although the fact that I bothered to think that means I felt uncertain. In any case, her poem surprises me. Her mother was way too much of a sophisticate to be the mother in the poem—she always reminded me of Anne Bancroft/Mrs. Robinson, in fact. Her older brother Jerry died at twenty of an overdose, but that was later. Or was it?

I flip around, looking for my own contributions, but there aren't many—maybe I was too engrossed in photography to bother with writing that year. It's too bad I didn't keep any of the pictures I took—maybe I would be able to look at them now without thinking of him. I don't remember destroying them, but I guess I did.

20
Nora

Looking at the evening sky through the library window, I try to remember sitting here with my mother. I used to do my homework at the desk here while she sat across from me reading—not every night, but sometimes. We used to talk a lot, back then. I told her everything—that I was taking LSD when I was sixteen, that I was smoking pot when I was fifteen—so I must have also told her that my teacher was having sex with my best friend, and that he had stuck his hand up my shirt in the darkroom.

I can vaguely, in the corner of my mind, recall a conversation she and I had about the man himself—a typical gambit of my mother's would have been to ask some "we're just adults comparing notes" question like, "Well, what do you think about this Rasmussen character, Nora?" Or, "Your teacher is quite the Lothario, isn't he?" But how would I have answered?

I picture us late on a Saturday morning, sitting at the kitchen table—the only table we ever used. I am drunk with sleep—so recently returned from my elaborate preteen dreamworld that I'm still angry at reality for being real. My eyes are swollen and the gray-white T-shirt I sleep in every night must smell like dirty bed linen, but my mother is oblivious to the dust, dirt, scum, and other slatternly manifestations of our apartment. It's too big for one single working mother to clean.

So there we are, me in my child's dishabille and she in her Moroccan djellaba—obtained while I was away at camp.

"So Mom," perhaps I said, "I don't know what to do about Beth. She's my best friend, my only real friend, but she's spending all her time with Rasmussen, and it gives me the creeps."

"What gives you the creeps?" my mother the therapist would have asked me.

"The way she acts around him, the way she looks at him. It's like she's a different person when he's around."

"Oh, she has a crush."

"You make it sound so juvenile. She just likes him and wants to hang around with him. It's just that most of the time that means at his house, listening to his stupid records or looking at his stupid books or playing with his kids, and none of those things are things that Beth and I used to do together."

"Well, maybe you need to learn to branch out a little, my dear."

She actually called me that, "my dear." It never sounded like a term of affection, though; it sounded more like "old chap."

"Are you saying I should become one of his pet girls, too?"

But no, I wouldn't have said that, either. I didn't call them "pet girls." "Teacher's pet" meant something different or, at any rate, impossible to align with that teacher and that classroom in that school. There was no one polishing apples for Rasmussen or trying to get a better grade. We didn't get grades—all our work had equal merit. We weren't even allowed to compete in "gym" (during which we did folk dancing, yoga, and relay races). Maybe being a Rasmussen groupie was a way for some of us to win at something—but then why didn't it appeal to me? I am as competitive as they come, as it

turns out, a constant comparer of assets and a greedy collec-
tor of defeats. I was almost fifty before I was able to identify
this trait, unfortunately. Back then my way of understanding
it was that I was "just insecure," or "had low self-esteem"—
suitable character flaws for a female—not even really problems to be solved. My mother, a child of lapsed Puritans, had
embraced psychological explanations. For her, it had been lib-
erating to admit to having complex emotions and a difficult
mind. For me, the habit of self-analysis is a trap.

So, what could I have said to Adeline about Beth and Rasmussen? "She's fucking him" comes to mind. I didn't often
say that word around my mother but if I did she would not
have scolded me. I would have said, "She's fucking him," to
make her see the gravity of my abandonment. I would have
stared at the battered edge of the breakfast table and picked
at the peeling white enamel paint. When I looked up at my
mother's face, she would have looked serious, her mouth an
unspoken "no."

"That's quite impossible."

"Are you saying I'm a liar?"

"No, I'm saying that, possibly, Beth has misled you or is
herself confused."

"But she's not the only one, Mom."

Her head is shaking from side to side, decisively. "Girls can
be extremely cruel and silly at your age."

"But what about him?"

"He told you this?" Finally, I see shock in her eyes but just
for a second. I am too young to pounce on this crack in her
denial, too invested in trying to get someone to see things
through my eyes, to acknowledge my truth. I didn't need her

to see him as a rapist, then; I needed her to see him as an agent in Beth's betrayal.

"You've met him, he's obviously a pervert"—she hates it when I abuse technical terms—"a sex fiend, whatever you want to call it."

"Darling, you can't tell that from the way someone looks on the surface. It's a very serious diagnosis."

"But he's always insinuating and making double meanings, he's always implying . . ."

"Implying is human nature. There's nothing to be done about *that*."

But why is she arguing with me?

Certainly, she knew her share of arrogant, domineering men. My grandfather was the king of them. What she couldn't imagine was that someone with Rasmussen's warp would be so unhidden, so obvious. But in 1971 there was no real need for him to hide: the sexual revolution had been a *Time* cover story, "Young Girl" was a top-40 hit, and the Canadian prime minister's marriage to a woman twenty-eight years his junior was celebrated as a triumph of flower power. I doubt that Adeline even saw the circumstances I was describing as something I might need to be protected from—she wanted me to be "free."

But I was born free, like Elsa the lioness. My troubles with men come from some other place—maybe just the place of bad luck. My last love affair, the one that threw me off the horse for good, was with a guy named John. It was unlike any other affair I've had as an adult because it lasted for almost three years and because I thought it would last forever. I thought I had found, in John, a mate who was my intellectual equal, who was honorable, and whose idiosyncrasies were unlikely to result in either of us getting badly hurt. And I'm not sure I was wrong about any of that. I haven't spent a lot of time deconstructing it. Our relationship ended before Adeline died and, for a long time after that, picking up the pieces of anything felt like a waste of time. My mother used to say I was incapable of intimacy, but I was intimate with John. I don't just mean that I had sex with him, or looked into his eyes (which he disliked), or even that I let him see me at my worst. I mean that I came to like the way his sweat smelled, that I didn't mind touching his dirty socks, that his humanness became part of my humanness.

It's now dark out and my feet are falling asleep from sitting cross-legged on the library floor. I carefully unfold each leg and wonder what to do with myself. It's not even seven o'clock. I hate this part of my day. I used to have friends, dinner plans, theater tickets, but now I'm too broke for any of that and I was never much for keeping up friendships on the phone. I lie down on my back and look at the ceiling: the star mural is much-faded now, but still there. *ALbemarle 5-4176*, I think. Beth's old number. She won't be there, of course, but maybe I can still catch her at work. I pick up the *Tis Bottle* and carry it back up the hall with me to the telephone nook and pick up the olive-green receiver, which feels impossibly cold and heavy. I dial 411 to get the number of Rachman Weeks from information. Thankfully, a human being picks up the phone there and transfers me over to Beth, who's still at her desk. When she answers I say, "I've been reading the *Tis Bottle*."

"Omigod, Nora! You still have it?"

"I do. It's quite a relic. I just read a poem you wrote, 'My Son, the Doctor.' It's pretty funny, do you want to hear it?"

There is a protracted pause and I'm not sure what's happening. I start to feel as though I've said something wrong. "Beth? Are you there?"

"Sorry, yeah. I . . . Where are you?"

"Home."

"Which is?"

"I figured you saw the number come up on your phone . . ."

She takes this in. "Really?" She is incredulous.

"Yeah. I inherited it. And I can't sell so I'm stuck."

"Adeline's gone?"

"About eighteen months ago."

"Can't sell because of the economy or some other reason? 'Cause if it's a legal thing, maybe I can help. It must be worth, what, seven million?"

I can't believe she just appraised my grandfather's apartment. I flash back to my meeting with the lawyers. "Don't even think about what it's worth," the lady had said, fingering her fancy gold pen. "It will just make you bitter." And she looked like she knew what *bitter* meant. I don't want to explain to Beth how my grandfather had this fantasy that his apartment was some kind of museum of himself so there's another weird silence until I say, "I shouldn't have called, should I? I mean, because of the case."

"No, that's not it at all. I'm just thinking, my husband's out of town and it would be so great to see you and really catch up. It's practically on my way home."

"Uh, don't come here. I mean, there's like no furniture. Or food. But I could meet you somewhere."

"Is Armando's still there?"

"Barely, but yeah. I think they're closing at the end of the month."

"Then we have to go there! Seven thirty?"

"Sure, see you then."

21
Bob

From: bear@nyc.rr.com
To: PBJ@nyc.rr.com
Date sent: Feb 19 2009 5:28PM MST
Subject: On the Road

So yesterday I picked up a hitchhiker. She told me a story I know you'll get a kick out of. I won't deny that when I saw her standing alone on the highway I thought she might be a runaway, but I wasn't going to do anything, you know that. Anyway, once she's in my car I see that she's a grownup, nineteen or twenty, at least. Running away from a man is my guess. She has no real destination. "I'll let you know when we get there," she says. She shuts the door and puts her hands in her lap so I can see the pale streak on her left ring finger. Rasmussen, right as usual!

"Do you mind if I smoke?" the hitchhiker asks me.

"Yeah, I do, and so do your lungs," I say, looking at her again, because she's given me an excuse to. "I used to smoke," I add, not wanting to be too much of a daddy. "It makes me crazy to smell it. Especially when I'm driving or . . . you know, other times." She nods, noncommittal, and we roll on into Monument Valley. The afternoon light on the mesas makes their surfaces look like those microscope pictures of internal organs or some special kind of velvet—but really it's like nothing else because what it does is make my brain shut the fuck up.

"If I'm not gonna smoke, we better talk," she says.

"Okay, you first."

"Shit," she says under her breath, caught in her own trap. Then finally, "Where are you from?" So she's smart, too.

"Nice maneuver," I say, "but it's not that easy. I said you start, so start. Why don't you answer my first question. Where are you going?"

"Someplace far enough my ex can't find me and country enough they won't call any references."

It's a tough speech but it comes out shy. She's forcing herself to keep going just because I said to. "So you've been through here a million times, I guess." She nods. "It's my first time through in twenty years," I tell her.

Ten miles later, we come up to my favorite stretch. "I was planning to stop up here by the white mesa, hike in, and take some pictures. I can understand if that's not what you had in mind."

"I'm not going to have sex with you," she says.

"That's okay, I'm married," I tell her. It turns out to be the right thing to have said, because she agrees to come with me. Well, the wrong right thing in your eyes, I bet. But you know she wasn't my type.

Her name turns out to be Rose. She tells me she was named for a character in a book she hasn't read. When I pull over, we're at a place where a small, climbable-looking mesa is near enough the road to approach on foot, and the light is turning yellow on its western face. "There." I point. "Are you game?"

"There may be snakes," she says.

"Bring your gun," I say, and she smiles. Her teeth are terrible, not just crooked but stained, badly repaired with a metal-framed veneer over one incisor. It makes her look a little like a machine. She's been hiding them up till now but the smile about her gun is genuine and large. She's definitely carrying.

She goes ahead of me and at one point loses her balance but just brushes the dust off her ass like some kind of dance she learned as a girl. And that makes me remember that time in 1971 when Daisy fell and almost went over the cliff at Bandelier. She wouldn't stop crying. Her face was torqued like an infant's and she was covered in that same powdery dirt. Naomi raided my cache of cold beer for a compress and kissed Daisy on the part in her hair like she used to kiss Doria. Then she calmed down.

Once we're out of sight of the road, I ask Rose to strip—I know what I'm doing, it's not a slip-up—and she pulls her button-down shirt over her head like it's a turtleneck. I see her whole body before she can see me seeing it. She has hard little tits and a bony ass, which I knew before she took off her clothes. But the whiteness of her skin where her clothes end surprises me. Somehow, instinctively, she knows how to pose without instructions, snuggling her whole body into a ridge where she says the sun's heat is still in the rock. Her skin is pebbled with goosebumps and the contrast between the softness of the stone and the stippled skin is perfect. I'll show you the shots when I get back.

On our hike back to the car, she's monosyllabic. Doesn't even ask if she can smoke again, though I can tell she's dying to—fidgeting and sighing. When we get to the road, I tell her,

"Have a cigarette, you're killing me." And she lights up, and turns her back to me, leaning on the side of the car like it's a horse or something. Then I sit in the driver's seat and watch her in the side mirror, the tiny orange light traveling back and forth from her hip to her mouth.

It's dark when we get to Colorado. I'm heading for Cortez—like getting there this time is going to overwrite the time I never made it. I'm getting all kinds of 1971 flashbacks: waiting for my father to bail me out in that pissy jail cell, wondering what would happen to me if he didn't, deciding I deserved it all, imagining how I would beg for forgiveness if he ever did show up. But he wouldn't even look me in the eye, and I was so low and so rank by then, I was past believing I could ever get right again—with him or anyone else. I was an asshole before that, but I wasn't the guy he thought I was then. Not yet. Anyway, you're not going to believe this story.

Rose says they knocked down the Big Indian motel ten years ago because—well, it was going broke, but she says one reason it was going broke was because of this local legend about the child molesters in the hippie van. In the version she tells, I'm six foot six, red-bearded to the waist, and have a harem of twelve girls in one tent, each of them stolen from a different town in the Navajo Nation. It's fucking biblical. I asked her where the motel fit in and she said the last anyone saw of any of the girls, an old white man with a bow tie was making them all get into a hippie van in the parking lot. She said all the girls in the Four Corners knew to look out for the orange van: I'm the boogeyman of the Navajo nation, and my old dead Pop's the Grim Reaper!

We never talk about that time, Peanut. I'd be interested in your version, what you remember. It's been a long time since you told me a story. Send me an email—I've decided to go see Archer at the state hospital. Yeah, you read that right. His sister got to me.

This morning, Rose was gone. I knocked on her door to tell her it was wheels up but the maid was in there already. I could tell she was ashamed of what she'd shown me on the mesa, her need to be seen. Funny because it's all I want half the time: just to look. And so often what girls want, too: to be seen. But when that transaction actually takes place, instead of everyone walking away satisfied, there's shame and name-calling.

The girl who first explained that to me, about girls, was your friend Nora. She had gray eyes that made the skin around them look purple in contrast and she could narrow them into one of the meanest looks I've ever seen on a girl that age. We were making prints in the darkroom. Her pictures weren't very interesting but at the time I was interested in her, in unlocking her. I put my hands under her T-shirt while she was adjusting the enlarger and she said, "What makes you think it's a good idea to do *that* right now?" She sounded forty-five years old, that kid. "Because you're beautiful," I said, which was usually all I needed to say. "You're a moron," she told me. "When you tell a girl she's beautiful, she knows you're trying to get something from her. If you just look at her like she's beautiful, she might actually believe you." Naomi was so afraid of her for a while—when she punked out of the trip at the last minute it seemed like she was going to blow the whistle. And then we got caught anyway. Still, she really could have fucked things up if she wanted.

22

Naomi

That night on the reservation campground was the longest night of my life. I stayed with the girls, put them back to bed, and sat up in the camper van trying to figure out what I'd do in the morning. For a while I played the radio down low. There was a country station like the one in Wheeling I used to listen to and I tried to soothe myself with "Help Me Make It Through the Night" and "(I Never Promised You a) Rose Garden." I waited until four—six back home—before I got everyone back in the camper van and set out for the pay phone in Kayenta to call Percy, who'd only ever hated me and vice versa. I could barely drive but the road was dead straight and the tar macadam fresh enough and I just pretended. The girls were too upset with everything else to realize they had a flat-out fool behind the wheel. When I got back in the camper van after the call, they were all sleeping like tops.

Pat picked up the phone in Connecticut. When she heard my voice at that hour she was afraid, of course, that her son was dead. I didn't call often. I told her he was fine, just in some trouble. Percy didn't need me to fill in the details—there'd been a girl before me, when Bob was seventeen and she was thirteen: Lee Ann. Percy had to sort that one out and he knew, like I did, that there was always another shoe to drop.

Still, I don't think he expected the whole harem. He said he'd meet us in Cortez by nightfall and he did. And he gave me his American Express card.

My job was to keep the kids in line at the motel, and to figure out food and what to tell their parents. I sat in a chair by the pool and carefully printed out the words I would say on the phone, big and clear like I did for the class mimeos. I printed them as though I could present those parents with a lovely scroll: *We hereby declare your daughters safe and clean and fed right. They got a bit shook up but weren't ever, ever in danger.* Of course Percy wound up calling the families, finally, but sitting there scribing kept me from putting my kids in a taxi and finding us a new life in Colorado—like that girl he picked up the other day. I never wore a marriage band so I wouldn't even have had that giveaway streak of missing tan. We would have made it.

My great fear at that time was Nora. She'd paid her deposit to come along with us that summer and her mother had signed the permission form. That was in maybe February or March. Then in May, she changed her mind. I was sure he'd gotten to her. And because she wasn't like the others, and I'd warned him as much, she'd not fallen in love but instead gone to brood. It seemed to me it was only a matter of time before she cried rape. I sat by the pool and worried about Nora, back in Brooklyn, the unexploded land mine. Even though he'd already got caught white-assed and red-handed, pantsless among the lilies of the field, I thought Percy and his checkbook could silence anyone. I bet there's a school or a community center out on that rez today that has the name Rasmussen on it.

It was two days we stayed at that motel. Other tourists came and went, but without my shaggy husband, there was nothing that noticeable about me and the kids and the girls. The girls had a fantastic time just laying out by the pool, reading the magazines other people left behind, watching TV in the room, buying cokes and candy for a nickel more than they were worth from the machine because I wouldn't let them off the motel lot. And for some reason, they obeyed: no sass, no rebellion. One of them—could it have been Beth?—brushed and braided my hair for me that first night. I had to pretend it tickled to hide how it made me weep to be tended to that way.

23

Nora

Armando's is an old-school, red-sauce Italian restaurant that Beth and I used to meet at when we were in high school—nobody got carded anywhere in those days, is my memory. I had my first cocktail there, a sidecar or some other curiosity I'd picked up from old movies on Channel 9. A zombie?

It's dark inside as I first enter. There's a bar up front, on my right, and the restaurant tables are farther back. Since there are exactly two people at the bar, both closer to the dining end of things, I position myself at the corner nearest the front door. Beth will have to turn her head to see me when she walks in, so I will see her first. I know she will be late. I order a Manhattan because it is something I will consume by the eyedropperful.

I am afraid of becoming a habitué of Armando's, that it's somehow my destiny to be transformed from the mostly unregenerate 1970s hippie kid I was until a few years ago to the boozy old broad who keeps carfare in her brassiere and leaves orangey lipstick imprints on an ashtray full of Newports. And who is that very specific person? Never my mother. More likely a character from a movie. But I fear she is inside me, that one cocktail will awaken her like those folded paper flowers that gradually bloom when you drop water on them. Beth taps me on the shoulder and I jump.

"Nora?"

I don't recognize her, but who else can it be?

"Beth?"

"Jill Goldberg. You don't remember me—I was a few grades behind you at the Academy. You look exactly the same!"

She's right, I don't remember her. I'm even a little suspicious of her claim. "What a funny coincidence," I say, without conviction.

"I just stopped in to kill a half hour before the show. May I?" she says, and takes the seat next to me.

"The show?"

"At Saint Ann's."

"Isn't that in DUMBO now?"

"No, the school. My daughter's in seventh grade. They're doing Hamlet!"

Okay, that makes sense. She isn't seeing a show at the avant-garde theater; she has a gifted child at the school for gifted children (we did a lot of sneering at them in the playground when they deigned to appear there) and they are putting on a play about adultery, suicide, parricide, and the perfidy of re-marriage. Brava! I say none of this, except "Wow."

The bartender comes by and Jill gazes at my drink, trying to determine whether one of the same is a good idea. I shake my head. "Vodka tonic," she says.

"Do you have kids?"

This is almost always an aggressive question so I have learned not to elaborate on my one-word answer. I am not in charge of making my childlessness palatable to the child-ridden. I find

I want to keep Jill Goldberg around, though, so I change the subject.

"It's funny, I'm actually meeting Beth Cohen in a few minutes—for like the first time in thirty years."

"You guys were inseparable!"

"BFFs, give or take an F."

"Ha," she says. "You're funny."

"We're forming a posse," I say, surprising myself considerably.

"A what?"

"A vigilante mob. Want to join?"

She looks at me hesitantly—but not as though my question is crazy, only as though asking, "Are you saying what I think you're saying?" Because although she was too young to have had Rasmussen for eighth grade, she is not too old to be outraged by what he did to us.

"What do you think?" I prompt.

"What's the plan?"

"I don't know. You're the first person I've told."

Her drink arrives and she clinks it on mine but she is scowling, slightly. Maybe she is thinking about her own daughter, wondering how much of the TLC she's getting at Saint Ann's school is just as tainted. I look at my watch—Beth is fifteen minutes late. In other words, she should be walking through the door any minute now. Jill takes my distraction as an opportunity to escape.

"I don't want to horn in on your reunion," she says, taking an immoderate gulp of her drink. She starts groping around in her purse, presumably for a business card. Over her shoulder, I see Beth walk in. We recognize each other instantly.

Then Beth makes a *qué pasa?* face about Jill—the ice blonde in a black cashmere coat who's stolen her seat. I return her look with what I believe to be no expression on my face and she comes toward us, surrounded by one of those postmodern fragrances: cinnamon, ink, some kind of metallic flower.

"And who's this?" she says.

Jill has finally found her card and gives it hastily to me. She turns to Beth and offers a bony, beringed hand.

"Jill Goldberg, Academy class of seventy-four," she says.

"Sorry to be late," says Beth. "My husband's away visiting family so I can shop without getting the third degree." She jiggles the shopping bag she's carrying from the fancy clothing store next door.

The bartender returns. "Can I get you ladies anything?"

"God I hate that, 'ladies,'" says Beth, looking into the bartender's eyes. "A Diet Coke."

Beth sits on my right and puts her shopping bag on the bar, effectively telling me, "I made you wait while I preened." She is and is not beautiful. The nose job has brought her closer to the American ideal but her face doesn't quite have enough structure to keep that illusion alive. Her hair is perfect, though: it looks like it was blow-dried ten seconds ago, and she acts like someone beautiful—the way she settles herself onto her barstool and rests her forearm on the bar, as though there is a camera at the entrance to Armando's. We have not hugged or kissed—we never did as kids but it's odd in contemporary female friendship terms.

Her glass of soda arrives and she smiles a new and fascinating smile at the bartender, apologizing for her previous glare.

Then she turns to us and says, "And you, Jill, were you also, shall we say, a friend of Bob's?"

Bizarre that this is the first thing she says. Are we still reading each other's minds, after all?

Jill shakes her head. "I had Zahler for eighth."

"Too young," I say. "Wait, that came out wrong."

"Too young to be in with the in crowd is what you meant, I think," says Jill.

"Such a different time," says Beth. "Even the way we talked." She sounds like she's narrating a PBS special.

"We were kids," I say.

Jill looks at her watch. "Anyway, I was actually just leaving."

"Her daughter's in a play at Saint Ann's," I tell Beth.

"People love that school." She rolls her eyes.

"Sadie's very happy there," says Jill. "It's changed a lot since we were kids." She polishes off her drink with a zeal that indicates something rotten in her own Denmark. Then she puts a twenty on the bar—excessive, but I'm not about to argue.

Beth smiles. "Nice to meet you," she says.

"See you around," I say, though I doubt we will even greet each other if I do.

After she leaves, Beth and I examine one another. It's the kind of competitive analysis that women are programmed to do—even those (like me) raised by mothers who never once asked any of the subtextual questions aloud: Is she fatter than I am? Is her hair dyed? Does she have a spouse and is he worth having? Does she look old? Whoever of us speaks first will disclose her own deepest insecurity so I will not say, "Nice ring," about the sapphire-and-diamond trophy she's flashing. I do wish I'd put on a different shirt—the one I'm wearing came from the thrift store and though the color is great, the collar is too narrow to be contemporary and too nineties to be vintage. My pants are from Housing Works, too, but they are Escada and fit perfectly.

"So when did your mother die?"

"It was a year ago in August."

"You're still in mourning," she says, and pushes out her lower lip in a subtle recreation of a child's pout. "I'm sorry. I really liked your mom." Is she the first person I've talked to who actually knew my mother—the same woman I knew? "I know she wasn't much of a mom, but she was kind of a hoot as a middle-aged lady. Right?"

I suppose that's true but it's not one of the first ten things I would have said about her. "What about yours?" I ask Beth, to get the focus off my sickly little family tree.

"Both dead since the eighties. It seemed like as soon as I left college they both dropped off but I guess it really took longer than that. My mom had uterine cancer. It took a while."

"I'm sorry."

"Yeah, it sucked."

"When did you come back to New York?"

"Come back?"

"From California?"

"Oh, God. My first marriage—disaster. I came back after that."

"So that's when you went to law school?"

"No, didn't get around to that until—long story. What about you?"

"I've been here all along, more or less." She looks sympathetic, as though I am admitting to something shameful, so I correct: "Not right here, but in the city. East Village, mostly. But tell me about your first marriage. I love a good disaster."

She wrinkles her nose. "I hated the suburbs. I felt stuck. No excitement. And things just . . ." She shrugs. "I had an addiction problem."

This is almost disappointingly banal. Who didn't? Well, me—I'm just slow-motion, can't-get-out-of-my-own-way self-destructive. "Did you go to AA?"

"Sort of." She makes a line with her lips, weighing how much to tell me. "You were always good with a secret," she says. "But this is like a secret from yourself—like your work self. Know what I mean?"

"Not only can I keep a secret, I am a black belt in keeping work and life separate."

"I was in the sex trade." She waits for me to react.

I'm not able to take this information in, really, until I realize I am trying to put her in hot pants on Tenth Avenue and she was much more likely in cashmere at the . . . I don't even know what fancy hotel bar. The idea of Beth getting paid for sex isn't actually that shocking, because she was doing that in some form in high school—blowing guys in the bathroom at Xenon, getting taken on private planes to places I couldn't even imagine. I'd never been out of the city then. I sometimes thought that she liked telling me about her exploits more than she liked having them.

"Like, for money because you were broke?"

"No. We had money. It was—'for thrills' sounds wrong. If you've never had an addiction it's kind of hard to explain."

The bartender signals *another round?* and I nod, immediately. "Your husband understood?"

She shakes her head. "I got roughed up one night—detached retina, broken rib—"

"Then you stopped."

"After my ex took away my son I stopped." I see her focus her eyes on the television set across the bar. Her face goes absolutely expressionless, sphinxlike.

"You have a kid?"

"Winslow," she says.

It takes me a moment to realize that's not some secret password—it's a name. I look at my own hands on the bar, always so much older-looking than expected. Winslow Homer? Winslow, Arizona? Win slow? Or is just one of those mock-cowboy names that doesn't mean anything? "Is that why you became a lawyer? To get him back?"

"I do that because I'm good at it." She looks at me with a sly smile, proud.

I nod. Fair enough. Most people's motives are not as direct or clear as I want them to be. It's not as though I can really explain my own path to the job I have or the life I'm living. And what about our perp, Harold Singer? Did he choose to become a teacher because he liked young girls or because he thought it would be more fun than working in an office?

"Did you read that poem she wrote—the first girl your client molested? It's like something straight out of the *Tis Bottle.*"

She looks back from the TV, confused by my leap. "No."

"I'm pretty sure she killed herself."

"That's sad. But see, you're blurring the line now." She means between work and her past—our history.

"Sorry," I say.

"Anyway," she says, "it's not like I think there's no such thing as a sex crime, it's just the way people think they're entitled to some abstract justice, some consensus version of right and wrong. I mean, nobody 'gets her story told.'" She makes air quotes. "A lawsuit doesn't do that for you. You see that every day at the ED. Right? Remember how you used to make fun of your mother's clients for thinking they could solve their problems by telling her about them? It's the same thing. What happened, happened. You have to figure out how you're going to live with it."

"And the perpetrators?"

"If there really was a crime committed, that's a different side of the street."

"What about Rasmussen?"

"What about him?"

"You don't hold him responsible for anything? In your life?"

"Don't be ridiculous."

"I don't know. It sounds like there might be a connection, don't you think? Between being molested by your teacher as a fourteen-year-old and becoming a prostitute?"

"Grow up, Nora. Do you blame him for making *you* an old maid?"

Oh, yeah, I forgot. Beth could be really mean. Teenage Nora would have told her to go fuck herself but as an adult I am speechless. And though the comment was awful, the look on her face is instantly regretful. "You never wrote me back," she says then.

She must have emailed me this afternoon, after I left to go to Everett's. "I left work early today. I had to run an errand."

In light of her last comment, I am not about to tell her about Tin Man.

"I mean in nineteen seventy-whatever. When I was losing my mind at New Paltz," she says. "You want me to blame Bob but you're the one who broke my heart." She stops drawing on the sweat of her glass with the edge of her perfectly painted, gray-beige fingernail and looks at me with unguarded eyes. I never knew her when she was that young—as young as the look in her eyes at this moment.

"I'm sorry," I say. "I just felt . . ." I can't say "like I was better off without you," which is what I did feel. "It was so long ago." But I don't have any trouble knowing what letter she's talking about. I've felt guilty about not writing back for thirty years or whatever.

"I forgive you," she says, putting her hand on my forearm, just for a microsecond—we both notice instantly how odd it feels. As she pulls back, I see a glint of silver at her wrist that I at first mistake for the Indian silver bracelet she got from Bob, but she's wearing a black suit and a mauve silk shirt and her hair is so perfectly blown out it shimmers, so it's probably a Swiss watch or a Tiffany bracelet or something.

"So anyway," I say, pulling my shoulder bag off the hook under the bar and removing the *Tis Bottle*, in all its battered glory, "I thought you'd want to take a look at this." She takes it from me cautiously and turns the first few pages with the flat of her palm, like a rare book. Her eyebrows are raised as she reads.

"Naomi's handwriting!" she says and then looks up at me. "This is such a blast! I can't believe you held onto it."

"It was in my grandfather's apartment," I say.

"You know, I bet I could get you out of that. Did I say that already?"

But she's distracted by something she's found and begins to read, smiling to herself. "Remember this?" she says, and starts to read:

"'Here lies Nora Buchbinder, fifteen-year-old weisenheimer. Buchbinder was best known for her Sears and Roebuck wardrobe choices and her prowess in "What's Wrong with This Picture?"...'"

I vaguely remember the write-your-own-obit assignment—other people's responses. Beth had imagined her future self a doctor; Trina was the first woman on the moon. But my decision to kill myself off as I was then strikes me now as creepy and disturbed. Beth seems to think it's just funny. "You were such a card," she says. I shrug. Then she closes the book, both hands flat on the cover. "I can almost smell it. The way the pages felt cold from the mimeograph when we first got them. The suspense about if my story would get picked."

"The obnoxious way he sang when he walked around the room handing out the pages," I say.

She laughs. "I'm sorry about what I said before. That was a cheap shot."

"It's okay."

"We should stick together. Old friends. We had to sing that corny song in Girl Scouts but it's actually true, it turns out. Right?"

"I didn't do Girl Scouts."

"Old rhymes with gold. Old friends."

I nod. I've finished my second drink and if I have another I will be a complete mess tomorrow. "I'm glad we did this," I say, although I'm not sure it's the truth.

"Me too," says Beth.

24

Peanut

From: PBJ@nyc.rr.com
To: bear@nyc.rr.com
Date sent: Feb 19, 2009 11:15 PM
Subject: WTF

If you think I don't remember August 1971, think again. I still call it the worst night of my life, in my head—though worse things have certainly happened. But since you asked, I'm writing it down. Maybe this is the right time for me to reconsider what happened to me then. Wouldn't it be funny if I started claiming to be a victim, too? You can take that as a threat, if you want.

In my version, it all starts with me boosting the bracelet. I have such a vivid memory of sitting in the front seat of the van, looking at it on my arm, thinking, *I can help myself to whatever I want.* Your disapproval really threw me for a loop, because I thought my intentions were obvious: I was staking my claim. You were worried about getting caught, I get that now, but I'm not even sure I was aware that we were breaking the law. I was such a dummy I thought "statutory" had something to do with "statues," that it meant that there was a Greek myth or something that was the original case of a man and a teenage girl doing it. Anyway, we were driving along and you saw the bracelet on my arm and yelled at me for ripping it off and I felt ashamed of myself, which was kind of a new feeling for me. My parents didn't have much energy left for scolding by the time I came along. I guess I liked it.

So we got to the campsite. I remember you made us call home and let our parents know we were changing the itinerary. Why did you do that? I remember the pay phones in a supermarket parking lot, waiting while the others took their turns. The place we wound up at was way, way down a dirt road with no hookups or showers or anything—on the reservation, I guess. It must have been. I don't remember much else about the actual place. We pitched our tents and ate our beans or chili or hash and went in for the night but you stayed out by the fire and I fell asleep before you came in. I remember trying to stay awake—pinching myself, kicking Tiddlywinks when she snored. We hadn't been on the road that long and there was still heavy competition about who you chose to sleep with, or next to. What I can't remember now, and I guess that means I "blocked" it, was hearing you fuck the others, or even your wife. I only remember how it felt to be with you in the sleeping bag, in the tent—the way it smelled and how hard the ground was, how the stupid air mattress just got in the way, how big and warm your body felt—much bigger than it did in the waterbed or anywhere we did it standing up, or whatever. And at first I would be performing for the others a little, trying to make it sound as dirty as possible, and then I would forget all about them and just be in a world of you. I was a stupid little shit.

I woke up to flashlights and yelling. "You there," they kept saying. And none of us knew which "you" they meant—we all thought we were the one who was going to be interrogated and go to jail. The light shining in our eyes and mean men yelling—like a World War II movie. I didn't realize the cops were Indians. To me they were just men in uniform, shouting—they were the pigs. You asked if they could point the light somewhere else so you could find some clothes to put on, but they wouldn't, and in the end you had to go with them in nothing but your T-shirt. You were yelling stuff over their shoulders to Naomi—who to call, where to go—but I wasn't listening. I was looking at your penis, which was suddenly tiny, like a boy's, hiding under your white, white belly.

How we got to the motel I can't tell you. Obviously, Naomi drove the van but I don't remember if it was that night or the next morning or what. I do remember seeing that place for the first time and being excited because of the neon sign and the swimming pool—for a minute, I thought it would all turn back into a vacation. Naomi must have taken over but I can't ever remember hearing her raise her voice, or speaking with anything but that ironical tone she had. I think it took like three days for your father to get there and bail you out, and get us all to wherever we flew out of. The plane was tiny, and I was scared of your strict, weird dad in his bowtie and his seersucker suit. Yeah, the Grim Reaper. That's not wrong. We changed planes somewhere, Denver, I guess. No one cried, except Doria, of course.

We got home in the middle of the afternoon. Everybody's parents were there and that was really weird. I'd never seen them all together in one place except maybe at my bat mitzvah. Most of the fathers I'd never seen before, at all. And they were all so mad. Well, mine was, that's what I'm remembering. I felt

bad for not having any souvenirs—as if what my father really needed at that moment was a plastic tomahawk. He looked
so fucking disappointed in me I guess I wanted to chop him
up. Mom hugged me but he just stood there with his arms
wrapped around his chest. On the way home he wouldn't even
turn on the radio for the Mets game. I remember waving good-
bye to your kids: "See you soon! Love ya!" I thought we'd be
reunited in a few days, weeks at most. And I thought *you* were
a political prisoner.

A political prisoner. Just want you to marinate in that a little. Like fucking Gandhi or something. That's how the mind
of a teenage girl works. Do you get it?

In September, when we heard about the settlement, that
we'd probably never see you again, we had a big sobfest at
Christmas's house, with Mateus rosé and Laura Nyro records, and I think Tiddlywinks even read some of her poetry. After that, we met once a week to reminisce and go over
the news, asking ourselves what you would have said about
the Yom Kippur War and "I am not a crook"—trying to stay
true to the "values" you'd taught us. We felt so abandoned—
by you, even though we knew that you had no choice; and
by our families, who treated us like lepers; and also by the
Academy board, who with all their liberal rhetoric wouldn't
stand up for our right to live and love freely the way we'd
been taught to stand up for everyone else's. *We shall over-
come*, my ass. That's what Uhura said, back when she was
hilarious. Our parents could have sent you away forever if
they'd pressed charges instead of agreeing to that settlement.
I guess it would have blown up the Academy, but still, they
could have.

So, instead of thinking about how your cycle of self-pity and etc. started then, why not think of 1971 as the year you didn't go to jail for the rest of your life?

I know you seduced that hitchhiker. I won't lecture you, because what's the point. I also won't let you back into this apartment. That was the deal, asshole.

25
Bob

From: bear@nyc.rr.com
To: PBJ@nyc.rr.com
Date sent: Feb 19, 2009 11:00PM MST
Subject: re: WTF

Here's my version:

I came back to our honeymoon motel to write it for you, because I love you and want you to remember how much, but also for Archer, because . . . I'll tell you about that later. I may be the lying bastard you think I am but at least I'll never do that to you. I don't mean shoot myself and leave a half-dead man behind, I mean force you to spend the rest of your life wondering how you fucked things up so badly, so completely, that forgiveness is beside the point. That's the irony. The worse it gets, the harder it is to pretend that there are such things as redemption or forgiveness, and the more I just want to say, "fuck it."

When I was twenty-six, looking at my son was like looking at the worst part of myself: the fear in his eyes all the time, the eagerness to please. I loved that kid more than I've ever loved anyone, even though I hated him, too. He was so clearly a copy of me.

Anyway:

Before I let you all out of the van, I give the talk: we're guests. We represent New York City, the East Coast, dirty hippie communists, right? Don't give them any more reasons to hate us than they already have. You say, "Don't lecture us, get a haircut," and Archer high-fives you. I pretend to laugh. But I know you'll all behave in this place, because it's cool. I say "One hour," and you scramble, leaving me, Naomi, and Doria, who's fast asleep at her mother's side. She's four. When she was nursing, Naomi used to say she felt like a cow but now she's more like a tree, rooted to the spot, nourishing, sheltering, all the while getting dryer and more rigid. She shrugs at me. "Go on in," she says. "They can't be unsupervised in there. Remember the kid at the counter?" And I didn't until this second. When we were here two years ago he was around your age, so he's sixteen or seventeen now.

I don't think I'll ever get tired of that place. Even the name—who says "topsy-turvy" anymore? I love that they've been leaving their kid in charge of the whole thing since he was Archer's age. I love that every time I come here it looks like it just got a fresh coat of paint. A lot of roadside attractions turn up a little sad if you come by a second time but this thing has a funny integrity. Inside the front room that serves as ticket booth, newsstand, and gift shop, the kid's come out from behind the register—he's already flirting his ass off with Trina, who's gazing at the silver bracelets in the dusty display case. "That's a pretty name, is it Spanish or something?" he asks, like he's never seen anything like her before. But no, everybody's got a TV. She's just Lieutenant Uhura in civilian clothes. I'm going to make that her nickname—it might come off racist but screw it. The rest of you are waiting by the bathroom.

I peel ten bucks out of my money clip, making sure the kid sees my watchband—Navajo silver and better by far than anything he'll ever sell. "A buck a head?" I say and he nods. "Two more in the car might join." Sometimes my speech goes all cowboy out here but I've got no legitimate claim to that.

"Is the little girl yours?" he asks me, trying to be friendly but meaning Archer.

"My son," I correct him and can tell he's flustered and embarrassed because he thinks he's too hip to make that mistake. "Happens all the time," I say. "We really need to get his hair cut but he won't let anybody near him with scissors."

I let you get a head start so I can surprise you in some way I'll figure out later and scan the Arizona Republic, biding my time by the door. This is the second most fun thing about traveling with girls—I can always get a squeal out of at least one of you. On a good day, I'll get pummeled by tiny, ineffectual girl fists or someone will walk off in a snit and require soothing. You don't see my tricks as the pathetic strategies of a seventeen-year-old boy trying to get laid. You don't realize twenty-six is no better than seventeen. The paper fails to mention the war, except for two death notices. Events in New York City are invisible, too. The teenager's leaving me alone here; he can tell I'm not a thief.

"Hey," says Naomi, who has slipped in without my realizing it.

"Where's—?"

"Asleep in the back. I left the windows open."

"Are you going in?" I ask her, really just wanting to know if my fun will be spoiled. Not that she ever gets in the way, or even comments, just that she observes—even with her hair in her eyes when she's pretending not to. It was what I fell in love with about her the day we met.

"Is it Italian or something?" she asked then. I was about to leave a buck on the counter and walk away when I realized she meant my bike.

"How did you know?" How did a waitress in Sherrard, West Virginia know an Italian motorcycle from a hundred yards away?

"It came up quiet. And the color too."

Babe the Blue Ox. Did I tell her that then? I don't know. I can't remember how I got her into my sleeping bag, or how it happened that she stayed strapped around my waist all the way back to Brooklyn, except that she kept on seeing stuff and clueing me in her matter-of-fact way—like I was some peculiar rock she'd picked up on the beach and couldn't decide whether to keep or send skipping away. I was such a nitwit I didn't even ask her how old she was. Then one day she came back from applying for a waitress job at Junior's and wanted to know what working papers were. She had those eyes put in with dirty thumbs; they made her look older.

In the first room, the Ames Room, I can hear Archer running—tearing back and forth through the plane of the illusion. He's chasing Daisy. She's finally stopped sulking over spending last night in the kids' tent. I realize she's flirting with my son—kind of makes sense, since she's a young fifteen and he's an old seven, but they never said boo to each other in Brooklyn. After seeing how much fun the kid's having,

Naomi nods toward the next room, the one with the chair on the wall but I'm torn—there are some fun ways to work the Ames Room illusion with a kid Archer's age. He'll love seeing me look small. Only he's not interested in Dad right now. I decide to bypass the chair and the uneven floorboards and go straight to the hall of mirrors, everybody's favorite. You girls are just on the cusp of being too old for all this but we've had two solid days of driving now and the drama of last night's choice of tents hasn't completely dissipated, either. I know it's sick to pit you against each other that way but you should really blame Nora for chickening out at the last minute. If she'd come along it would have been her, Naomi, and the kids in one tent and my girls with me, in the other, like every other summer we've done this. The current configuration just doesn't balance so there's been way too much horse-trading going on. I need to draw the line but I haven't. Drawing the line ain't my strong suit.

My plan for the mirror maze is to come in sidelong and get halfway down the first alley before you notice, and then start yelling, "Keep turning left," which is the wrong advice, of course. But what I'm not prepared for is that four girls jump out at me, led by Christmas. She has a sneaky side—like the time she pulled me into the ceramics room and let me walk out with her wet gray handprint on my face. Anyway, when I come around the first corner what I see is a bevy of maidens, infinitely reflected. It's dazzling. I wish I could freeze the moment but my camera's in the van and anyway then you scatter, chanting "Two, four, six, eight, who do we exasperate? Three, six, nine, twelve, who's too old to be an elf?" which you seem to have invented last night at the campsite and all find hysterical and that does exasperate me so the moment turns dark as fast as it went bright. This is the hell of girls.

Then you wander over to me and put your hand in my back pocket. "Gotcha!" you say but not with any malice. We stroll down the aisle of our reflections: four of us, eight of us, a kaleidoscope of big Swedes and coal-haired Peanuts uniformly blue in denim and chambray. And now my cock is pounding. You break from my side as we turn the next bend and see the other girls at the funhouse mirrors. Without hesitation, you angle your head in sideways for a beat and make an alien noise: "Oop!" The other two, who had been lamely plié-ing and waving their arms, instantaneously get the game and the three of you become a calliope or maybe a Swiss clock, jerking in and out of the frames of the three mirrors—fat, thin, and wavy—and bleating silly sounds—urk, gank, plork. It's not the play of little children but it's sure as shit not something three adults would spontaneously invent. You have no sense of being observed, and for a little while the cadence is effortless. Then you start to giggle and it's done. Tough luck. The kid from the gift shop has loped over to gawk and the idiot says to me, "Got any pot?"

"Are you insane?" I ask him in my father's driest, meanest voice. "Do you want us all to go to jail? They're minors! I'm their teacher! Get out of my sight." He steps back but without any real sense of urgency. "Get your hair out of your eyes and pay attention," I say then, in a reasonable voice. I'm trying to erase the burst of Percy that came before but the kid yells back, "Get your sluts out of my funhouse!" before closing the door on me and my retinue. I don't know if my son knows what a slut is—but I want to protect him from the implication of something sordid.

We're back in the van no more than two minutes when Doria starts crying. I glue my eyes to the road and am inventing the evening's campfire story when you say, "Look!" but not like "Look, a deer!" or "How beautiful!" but more like "I finally got the math problem right!" and you are holding up your left forearm and waggling your hand to call attention to the silver bracelet on your wrist, stolen. You're one of the club with Naomi, and Christmas, and Tiddlywinks, and I consider turning around and making you return it then and there. But you are so proud of yourself and that kid was such a creep so we take it on the lam. I gun the van up to 70, heading north. You think you're smarter than the rest, Peanut. You look at me like a dog looks at meat. You're fourteen, baby, cut it out.

I'm not going to write about what happened at the campsite, or the jail, or the settlement. You've got your memories and there are public records, if anyone cares. I've tried to make amends in various ways but the damage is done. What I'd like you to remember is that I loved you. You, Peanut; and Naomi and Doria and Archer. Back then, all I wanted was that my son not grow up to be like me.

26

Naomi

In his version, I was barely just a coal smudge, a girl from a Dickens book. In my version, I saw him coming a mile off. Not him, specifically, but he was neither the first nor the last draft dodger from the East Coast on a motorbike, or in a VW bug, or whole families of them in camper vans. . . . Since I worked the counter that summer, I met a lot of them—even if they just came in looking for the john they talked to me. I had long hair that hung in my face like theirs did. I looked like I might be a member of their tribe. I knew it, too. I was shy, never said a lot, but I watched and listened and kept close track so when that big strong man with the fancy watch and the Italian motorbike showed up I was ready. I tied up the corners of my plaid shirt high on my ribcage. I said "far out" and asked for a ride. I said I didn't need a helmet because I wanted to feel the wind in my hair.

The ride up to the lookout point turned into a game of hide-and-seek at the table rock. When he asked me how old I was I knew he'd take me. He asked me if I knew any local folk songs and I said, "Like *Little Omie*?" But he didn't even get it—that it never ends well for the girl in the song who goes along with the stranger from out of town. "Come go along with me," says the stranger. "Have mercy on me," says Little Omie, too late.

27

Nora

I am in bed in my mother's old bedroom at the back of the building with a view of the water, and the Statue of Liberty, and the gaudy splendor of Lower Manhattan. Sometimes it's hard to close my eyes with the lights off because the view out the windows is so stunning. During my mother's lifetime my bedroom (the maid's quarters, officially) was at the opposite end of the apartment but, when I came back last year, I couldn't stand to sleep with the toile wallpaper and the corkboard plastered with postcards from friends I no longer know. So I installed an IKEAn bedroom suite, adopted a cat, and made Mom's room mine.

At least she did me the favor of dying quickly. I put it that way because I can hear her saying those words—I have heard her saying them in my head for over a year, pointing out that she did at least that much right and thereby half-acknowledging all that she did not, but without actually apologizing or listening to my side of the story. Again, this is all in my head. I'm not saying my mother was a horror. She wasn't. But her life was not about me and I resented that. I resent it still, which is why I keep her so far back in my thoughts and why I truly haven't mourned or even gone through the motions: no funeral, no paid obit. I put all the condolence notes in a drawer without opening them. I don't know that I ever will. It's enough that I live in this haunted apartment, where every doorknob knew her hand and every window, her gaze.

At a party, not long before she died, I met a soft-faced woman in her sixties and we wound up talking about some book or movie or story in the *New Yorker* that centered on a fraught mother-daughter relationship. And there was a moment of resonance between us when we looked at each other and knew that we'd been imprinted by the same flavor of momness. And then she asked me how mine was, because I was obviously of an age when moms may decline and I said, "Fine," and she said, "Just wait." The remark dropped between us like an anchor. Struggling to stay social, I said I'd heard the difficult ones were sometimes the hardest to lose and she nodded and then put her hand on my forearm and said, "I didn't think I was going to survive it." I left soon after and, walking to the subway through the West Village, I kept thinking that, no matter what I said or didn't say or did or didn't do, now I was going to have to suffer my mother's death like I had never suffered anything before. Because of this stranger's curse.

And when I got the phone call from Bellevue (she'd been admitted the night before but hadn't called me and the next night died alone, of a fistula), the first thing I thought of was that woman with her little paw on my arm and her long shadow. I swore to myself then that I would not be its victim, that I could prefer not to, like Bartleby, my patron saint of clerkdom. And for the longest time all I really felt was furious. An eighty-two-year-old woman checks herself into the hospital with mysterious abdominal pain and doesn't call her only living relative? Maybe she couldn't face me because she knew I was about to find out the real punchline—that she'd never made a will, leaving me trapped in the terms of my grandfather's. It's not like I lived in a different time zone or we were estranged. I talked to her once a week, at least, about nothing. Neither of us was under any illusion that we enjoyed it but my period of not speaking to her at all had been over for five years at least. (That was when I found out that my father hadn't actually died in 1963, she'd just thought that was the "easiest" thing to tell a seven-year-old.) But I had gotten over that, if not exactly forgiven it, and had even since then told her I loved her once when she was going in for some crazy surgery on her nose that required general anesthesia. I remember the sick feeling of suspense while I waited for the surgeon to report success, even though it was about as low risk as surgery gets, and the profound, physical relief when it was over because I did love her—then, anyway. It does seem that I do not love her now.

We had an epic fight when I was fourteen or fifteen. I don't know what it was about but we were screaming—standing in the hallway that runs the length of this apartment, the "alimentary canal," she called it. I understand now, a little, how a teenager winds up shrieking the way I was ("You're so oblivious! So helpless! It makes me sick to be seen with you!") but not her adult parent—and Adeline was giving as good as she got ("What makes you think I like living with you? Do you think I have a choice?"). One of us was on her way out, late for something. In my memory, I am both of us it seems. Anyway, as we yelled and wept and threatened, our then-cat Anna came out of my mother's bedroom, meowing in her most demanding voice: *Feed me! Feed me now!* But she did not head for the kitchen, she just sat at my feet and looked up, vocalizing. Her wailing cat-face is framed perfectly in my mind's eye. And when even that didn't stop us, she stood up on her hind legs and put her paws on my thigh. *I can't bear another second of this*, she said in perfectly comprehensible terms. *I will not stop my yowling until you do. I will not stop pretending to be human until you remember that we are a family.*

For a moment I forget that Tin Man is gone and I look for him. I am ready for sleep and for most of the past year he has lain next to me, in the crook of my naked body, at night. I would tell him that I loved him and that he was "the best cat in the world" and "my cat boyfriend." But apparently even that is more than I get to have, right now. Stop it. *Stop feeling sorry for yourself, Nora* is what my mom would say.

I'm in no condition to sleep, so I open my laptop. I find myself looking up the legal age of consent in New York State in the 1970s. I want to know what the law was back then, but this is not so easy to find and I get sidetracked reading a message board where men—among them admittedly registered pedophiles—research what's legal in their states of residence, what they can get away with. And there, some comment cites a long thread on Reddit started by a user with the handle "iforgivemypedodad":

I was one of the last people he talked to. He was bawling, practically screaming, "Do you still love me?" And when I said I did, he said, "You're just saying that because I'm your dad." He was

*beyond shit-faced drunk. The next morning, he went to work
but he never came home.*

This makes me start thinking about the Rasmussen kids,
Archer and Doria, and without too much effort I find that
Doria Rasmussen has a blog. *From Ancient Grease*, it's called.
The About Me section says: *I am a married woman of faith
living in a small city near the Rocky Mountains. I like to cook,
sew, read, eat, write, and garden. My husband is blind. When
I was little, I asked my mother where my name came from, and
she told me it was from Ancient Greece but I had no idea what
that meant.*

When I last saw Doria in person she was four or five,
with Shirley Temple curls and a truculent stance—a bit of
her daddy in miniature. But the last time I saw her was in a
photograph in the *New York Times*. She was getting married,
wearing what looked like a black negligee. She had an anchor
tattooed on her right bicep with her husband's name in it. I
can't help but wonder if that anchorman is her partner out
there, and if his blindness was the result of some accident in-
volving propellants and fire. Their wedding announcement
appeared in the Vows column—my mother pointed it out to
me, saying, "Look at this. Rasmussen. Same family?" as she
lobbed the section across the library. And I remember being
as amazed that my mother remembered Bob's last name as
that she apparently read the Style section (so lowbrow). But
she read everything, really. If the *New York Times* was a roast
chicken, there would have been nothing left to feed the cat.

The page of *Ancient Grease* that I have landed on is from
Thanksgiving 2007, right around the time my mom died.
Doria writes:

This was my first Thanksgiving without Mom and it was painful. Ray and I haven't figured out any particular traditions of our own and, for various reasons having to do with who my husband is, the burden of inventing new ones is on me. You wouldn't know it to see me but I grew up in something like a hippie commune in New York City. On Thanksgiving, my dad made us listen to a tape recording of Navajo prayers before we could start eating. Eventually, the cassette wore out—we could hear it fluttering and wowing before it broke. I think that was the last time I gave my brother a high five. The food we ate was normal enough. My mom grew up in West Virginia, "where men are angry, women are angrier, and food comes in cans." She wasn't up for vegetarianism or bean sprouts but she learned to make all kinds of things over the years. Four or five years ago, she started doing this onion tart that I may resurrect after she's been gone a little longer. I still miss her too much to try.

Naomi may be the one I have the most questions about—the one who could have explained Beth to me. She just vanished at some point, it seems like. But from Doria's description it sounds like she's dead. I resume reading:

I talked to my dad for a few minutes. Since he got remarried, he always invites us to come visit for the holidays. After ten years of "no," you think he'd get the picture but that's not how he operates. If you want to draw a line with him you have to grab him and shout in his face—and his hearing is fine, that's not the problem. From my point of view, it's a miracle that I can even speak to him but he doesn't believe in miracles. I think he does regret, maybe even repent, his sins, though. I'm the one who needs to learn to forgive. I am a slow learner. He always said that. He was joking but it wasn't funny.

You probably wouldn't expect Ray to be an amazing cook, but he is. He likes me to read to him from Bon Appétit, *and to describe the pictures in detail. He corrects me all over the place—my bad pronunciation of French words and also weird ingredient names I've never heard anyone say out loud: mirepoix, asafoetida, chiffonade. He also corrects my descriptions of the photos—which is so cool it's almost creepy. Like when I say whipped cream and he knows it's really meringue or I say pork roast and he says "loin." And then I tease him and say, "Okay, pork loin roast," and he says, "Roast pork loin," and I say, "Let's just call it Porky Pig in a pan," and we think it's hilarious.*

My husband is black. I don't know why I add that. I don't think I've ever mentioned it here before. Believe it or not, it almost never comes up, even though where we live, an interracial couple could stop traffic. But his blindness seems to unblackify him for people here somehow. Anyway, everyone in our faith community knows us as us, and Ray has never complained about racism to me, ever. He likes to say I'm in charge of complaining for the family. Mom cried the first time she heard him say that—all three of us were on the phone and she went quiet. It took me a minute to realize what was happening but Ray was already gesturing at me—fist to the eye like a baby. I asked her what was wrong and she said she was embarrassed that she didn't protect me enough when I was little. It surprised me but I saw how she got there—she was thinking my role as designated complainer was because I had a backlog of complaints, but that's not what Ray means when he says it. It's just that I'm the one who brings the dented cans back to the supermarket for a refund, or who gets the supervisor on the phone when there's something wonky on our credit card bill. Mom had so much guilt but she

was really the one who was the victim. I got bullied and humil-
iated but that's part of childhood. Who was protecting her? I
guess that's why I can't forgive my dad.

Some Thanksgiving post. I meant to write about the fantas-
tic meal that Ray made: duck with macerated cherries, potatoes
and parsnips a la russe, roasted brussels sprouts with hazelnuts,
and cornbread with anise seeds and cardamom. It was not the
kind of food that kids like so it's just as well we don't have any.
Afterwards we sang together at the piano. Some hymns and
some show tunes—no Navajo chants. I felt blessed.

Doria has posted some pictures—not of the meal but of
herself and Ray on vacation, and of their wedding in some
neutral American backyard. I can see that her curls and freckles are gone and her body is now cocooned in fat. Her husband
looks genial and happy, with an afro larger than one generally
sees these days and a kind of Fu Manchu beard—I guess he is
in charge of being beautiful for both of them the way she is in
charge of complaining and reading recipes aloud.

Even if her father never touched her, Doria's second life
makes a kind of sense to me. The only safe way to be around
that guy, if you were female and under the age of twenty, was
by being fat or ugly (or, in my case, mean) and she seems to
have belatedly and willfully become both. I say "willfully" because this was not the case when I saw her picture in the *New
York Times*. She was then aggressively sexy—I was shocked by
the idea of it, getting married in a black slip, her hair a wild
nimbus, her features outlined and exaggerated by makeup. It
seemed politically regressive to me. Bad enough to sell your
soul into marriage but to show up dressed like a cartoon

hooker and have yourself branded like chattel? Tattoos were still unironic then.

I browse the rightmost column of *Ancient Grease*, looking through the list of recommended blogs for anything that sounds like it might belong to a family member, but it's a mix of craft stuff (*A Dress A Day*), political stuff (ye olde *Talking Points Memo*, *The Washingtonienne*), and religious stuff (I can't even look). She may be a churchgoer but she has not abandoned politics. Further down the page are links to her past entries going back to February 2004, which is early in blogdom, I think. So that's interesting, too. She married a blind black guy, retreated to Wyoming or Colorado or wherever she is, got fat, and became an internet geek. I tell myself I dodged that bullet, but it's not even a bullet and there was never a point in my life where I could have made any one of those choices. And besides, she sounds happy.

28
Naomi

She is happy. As happy as anyone is. It's no small thing, that.

29

Nora

One of our writing assignments in Rasmussen's class was to compose a protest song. As an example, he provided us with a mimeo of a song written by a girl from a previous class. He didn't name the author but I suppose we each deputized our own favorite of the older girls. The song was called "Freedom," and it seemed to me then to be of Bob Dylan quality—not that I actually knew Dylan's work very well when I was thirteen, but I was full of opinions. The chorus, which I can still sing, was:

> *You say I got freedom, that I'm able to fly.*
> *But my baby's at war, and I still don't know why.*
> *There's blood in the streets everywhere that I look.*
> *And what you call freedom's just a word in a book.*

It mentioned her boyfriend's draft number, his decision to not flee to Canada, how her letters aren't replied to, and it even got around to the secret war in Cambodia ("Phnom Penh" rhymes with "lion's den," of course.) Anyway, it was pretty good for a kid, and unique in my experience not only for being from a girl's point of view but for completely avoiding the weepy part of love. The singer sounds proud of her "baby," and disgusted by her country at the same time—we discussed this.

The "you" she's addressing is America (or Amerika, as we liked to spell it then).

The following week, after we'd all finished our own protest songs, Naomi came to school with her guitar and set some of our efforts to familiar folk tunes. And then the two of them sang "You Say I Got Freedom" as an encore and we applauded with delight. After that, maybe years after, I changed my theory and decided that "Freedom" was really Naomi's song. Her handwriting was just too good for someone who didn't also take pride in the words she wrote.

Later, I was a counselor at the same summer camp I'd gone to as a kid—the campers were mostly rich Jewish kids from the suburbs. And though the camp was liberal-minded, it was not exactly integrated: most of the kitchen staff were black and everyone else was white, except for one counselor, Reggie, who was black but from Scarsdale—what we used to call an Oreo. Every night after dinner, he played basketball with the waiters, Tommy the cook, and two or three other counselors. It was a rowdy game with a lot of trash talk—mostly from the college kids. The basketball court was made of red clay, and it stuck to their sweaty clothes and made them look like that guy at the Columbia University protests who'd painted himself red to represent the blood of the Viet Cong.

One night that summer, we had a campfire and, as usual, the guitar counselor started things off. After the kids had yelled their way through "There but for Fortune" and "Long Black Veil," he announced something special and up came Reggie, grasping his own guitar by the neck. It was late in the summer and his afro had grown so long it flopped over into a side part, like an apple with a wedge removed. He flashed us a sly smile as he tuned up, and said, "This here's one of my own." The first words he sang were, "You say I got freedom, that I'm able to fly." At first I was confused, but then I decided that his original composition would come later in his set and by the time the second verse came around I had chimed in, proud of myself for remembering so much of a song I'd only heard once. But as I sang out, heads around me turned and eyes glared. Afterward, another counselor hissed at me: "What were you trying to do to him?"

"I thought I'd heard it before," I said, lying even before I had decided to.

She shook her head, disgusted. Apparently, she believed Reggie was the true author of the song (why wouldn't she?) or, actually, what she seemed to think was that he really wasn't the author and that he had stolen it—and therefore what I had done by singing along was call him out on that. It was the early days of political correctness. As outraged as I was by being falsely accused of racism (for this, really, was the charge), I also knew immediately and completely that I had nowhere to take my argument. Rasmussen baited me into this kind of thing all the time. So then I told myself another version to make myself feel better: Reggie really *had* written the song. And the girl from Rasmussen's earlier class had stolen it from *him*—he had broken up with her at a different camp and she wanted revenge. Or, maybe she just heard him singing it in Washington Square Park and changed a few words on the subway home. Maybe the song was really an old song with many versions and this was just one stop on its journey. But I find I am attached to the idea that it was actually Naomi Rasmussen's song. I want her to have had something of her own, that no one could force her to share or surrender, written in her own hand.

30
Nora

Very late at night the phone rings. At first it rings in my sleep and then my mother's voice comes on, echoing in the carpetless hallway. I wake up instantly, as though now is the moment of her dying, and only I can rescue her. Or am I thinking of Tin Man? In any case I rush to the phone and pick it up. On the other end I can hear breathing, or maybe sobbing. A woman's voice says, "Nora?" and I say, "Yes?" and then it sounds like she has put the phone down. Her voice is far away and I don't understand what she's saying. "Endless" or "helpless"? "Sucker punch"? "I hate you," is clear though, said in a lower register. I think it's Beth but I also wholly reject the idea. For all her troubles, I don't think she could be this person. But who is this person? A random stranger who knows my name? Whoever it is hangs up, and I go back to bed, badly shaken but soon asleep again.

Friday
February 20, 2009

31

Nora

I wake up late, feeling ruined, as though I have been running laps in my sleep, so I skip coffee, put on most of the same clothes I was wearing last night and run out the door still in a quasi-sleep state. It's a brilliant clear day, the first in weeks, and when I step out of my building and see the brownstones across the street with their details etched by the river-reflected light, I am suddenly grateful for belonging here.

I scan Montague Street avidly for signs of my missing cat as I walk. There are so many things along the way that seem to have been here my whole life: the polished brass water main, the dented and overpainted fire alarm call box, and the lost glove impaled on the cast-iron fence all echo back through time. Across Hicks Street, the Thai restaurant occupies the storefront where I used to gaze at Barbie outfits and molded plastic kits for manufacturing replicas of characters from *The Mummy*, *The Bride of Frankenstein*, etc. Back then, monsters were big business—and not human. When I look down at the pebbly surface of the sidewalk, I know how it felt when my roller skates encountered the smooth softness of bluestone after this aggregate, which is called "Cosmocrete" or maybe "Cementine." (The brass badges that brand the pavement are still here, worn almost illegible, but I know what they say.) I must have been a happy kid at some point because these waves of nostalgia knock me sideways sometimes.

In my head I see snapshots of the way Montague Street looked to me in 1971. Inside Ebinger's Bakery, the women with white collars wrap boxes in red-ticked string fed from a device on the ceiling and cut with a special ring worn on their index fingers. In front of Bohack's, a man unloads fruits and vegetables from a dark green truck, and across the street, the shoe repair guy in his blue apron smokes a stubby cigarette, awaiting customers. He frightens me but I don't know why. Further up, after the intersection, is Prana, the newly arrived hippie store, which contains all the clothes in the world that I want but can't have, as well as incense, posters, and—I suppose—drug paraphernalia. And past that is the store where we buy my Buster Brown T-shirts and underpants from the grumpy Italian woman who can tell my current size without measuring tape. Then there's Meunier's, where we buy presents—silver jewelry and onyx eggs, and, at Christmas, little brass candle holders whose flames cause silhouetted angels to spin and strike a tinny bell. All these experiences are linked by the elusive presence of my mother, whose scent I am following as she shops and browses and flirts. Once I saw her coming toward me and didn't recognize her, in her fully lipsticked and coiffured state, on her way to meet a man— although she never told me that in so many words.

The window of the downstairs Chinese Laundry still displays an illustrated ad for "Martinizing." Inside, the ring-shaped, firefly-green lighting fixture is just as it was, although I don't recognize the woman toiling beneath it. One of my earliest memories is of being left alone in there with her, the lady who didn't smile. Her eyes met mine, but her gaze was like the bathtub drain—not enough of a force to suck me in, but a definite emptiness, a pull. She'd nodded when my mother had asked her whatever she'd asked her, but she hadn't smiled then either. She stepped back from the steam-producing thing she had been operating and began tallying things on the abacus, glancing back and forth between it and the pile of clothes she'd just pressed, and occasionally over at me on the bench by the entrance.

The floor of the laundry is paved with black and white tiles like the ones in the bathroom at home: hexagons. My grandfather taught me that word. I focus on the smell—a powdery, incense-y smell that I think of as "rice," though rice never tasted that way. The lady's clacking continues as I begin to wonder if I am being punished for my behavior earlier in the afternoon when I refused the ponytail my mother wanted me to wear. She was angry. We were late, she said, though I had no idea what for. I look out the window to scan the street for her lavender coat. Instead, I see the deaf boy. He opens the door of the laundry and greets the lady with one of his strange roaring noises. Then he turns toward me and, with a knowing nod, roars again. I stare at the Band-Aid-colored box that nests in his shirt pocket. I imagine it sends him the awful noises he repeats as speech. "Deaf" is not something you get if you eat food off the floor or swim in a public pool; it's more like Chinese or Catholic, something that is part of you. But unlike Chinese or Catholic, deaf is terrifying.

My mother stops and speaks to this boy at length sometimes, nodding at his answers as though she understands them. He is a neighborhood character, like Sal the butcher, or Anya the German babysitter, or Leopard Lady, who teeters around in high heels, dresses in wild-animal fabrics, and laughs a screeching laugh that makes me hide in the playground bathroom, even though it smells horrible. Once I saw a streak of blood on her stockinged calf. The deaf boy accepts a box of shirts from the laundress and nearly dances out of the store, winking at me as he goes. And as the jingling door shuts behind him I know that I have been sitting in the Chinese Laundry too long. The lady comes over and sits down next to me on the bench, bringing the rice smell with her. I want to hug her but her grim expression puts an end to that. What if my mother never comes back and I have to stay at the laundry forever, like some kind of store cat?

The lady's bony brown hand creeps onto my knee. She just gives me a quick pat, more a tap than a pat, really. "Go to sleep," she says in a tired voice. The afternoon sun is coming in from the shop window and it warms my shoulders like a tiny shawl. I lie down on the bench.

I hear the jangle of the door as it opens to admit my mother, a tiny slender woman whose cloud of Pre-Raphaelite hair and lavender velveteen coat give her the allure of a rare flower.

"Well, look at you, snug as a bug in a rug," she says.

"Sleeping good," says the lady.

Did that really happen? Did my mother leave me at the Chinese Hand Laundry so she could meet a man? I can't believe that about "my mother," but I can believe it about Adeline.

The problem of crossing Court Street brings me back to the present. There is a narrow ravine through the filthy snow and though its banks are hazardous, there are too many New Yorkers trying to cross here for anything as civilized as queuing to happen. I am teetering along over the ridge when gravity catches me for a moment and I almost fall, which is a sensation worse than actually falling: the rush of adrenaline, the sense of imminent disaster. Can a person be trapped by memories? Harmed?

I pick my way carefully across the ice-glazed flagstones in front of Borough Hall and down the uneven stairs that flank the courthouse till I am on the windswept shore of Adams Street, waiting for its interminable light. I crossed this street for fifty-something years without knowing its name—no one lives here. At the traffic island, I look over my left shoulder at the mirage-like Empire State Building in the distance. *Hello, old friend.*

In front of the tall building in which I work, a twenty-foot-tall inflated plastic rat has been placed to remind visitors that the building's owners are hiring non-union electricians. When I was a freelancer I used to hesitate and worry before I crossed a rat-line (which is not exactly a picket). Now that I am a union member I blow right by, although I do still smile at the enormous ugliness of the thing: I think the person who invented the inflated rat was a genius.

In the elevator, I press 28 and unzip my coat. I am lucky I don't have to work amid the ancient file cabinets and shrieking steam pipes of Livingston Street or in that 1970s dump on Court Street, where the forty-year-old vertical blinds make the windows look like they're full of skeleton teeth. Our office has late-model Steelcase cubicles, clean bathrooms, and a wraparound view of the harbor. In Manhattan, an office with a comparable view would be housing a law firm or an investment bank (I temped at places like that, back when I could afford to not have health insurance). At the Education Department they buy off-brand Post-its that don't stick, and the water coolers are usually dry, but I can see three bridges and the Statue of Liberty, not to mention New Jersey.

32

Nora

On my chair is one of those big interoffice envelopes that's sealed by a piece of red string wound around a cardboard button. It contains a manila folder—a case file—with a typewritten label on its tab. The label says: Harold, Singer—a classic data-entry mistake. Clever Shonda Deville has had the perspicacity to check not just the name of the teacher I requested, but its inverse! I forgive her for her email stationery and cursive font.

The only things in the folder are a hearing decision from March 1999—a case I hadn't known about till now—and a much-copied form indicating that the rest of the file's contents have been removed under some subparagraph of the teachers' union contract. The decision says that, in the case of *Sarfati vs. NYCED*, although Singer showed poor judgment, there was no evidence of sexual impropriety, and he had shown adequate remorse. His job and salary were restored to him.

I log into my computer and open my email. At the top is a message from Beth, from last night. "My client accepts your offer of immediate retirement plus fifty thousand dollars. Please prepare the stipulation for expedited handling." I didn't say fifty and she knows it, but still, it seems she must have thought we already had a deal when she came to meet me last night and I feel guilty about that. Then it comes back to

me: that phone call. It must have been four in the morning—
did that happen? Was that really her?

My heart is actually beating faster as I swivel back to the
part of my desk that has been overtaken by paperwork. I
start putting things in piles, trying to think through what
my options are. Three strikes is not an argument, I realize,
but finding out about this earlier case has re-re-re-convinced
me that Singer should not be anywhere near a classroom. I
call Beth.

"What about this case from 1999?" I say when she answers. She doesn't miss a beat.

"That girl should never have been in public school. I think
they just put her there so they could sue. You know they do
that, right, the Orthodox?"

"Use their teenage daughters to entrap rapists? How would
that even make sense?"

"Ask your coworkers in Special Ed." (She means the families who sue the city for failure to provide special education
services in Yiddish every year, and then fund their religious
schools with the settlement monies, but this is the very defi-
nition of a red herring.)

"I know all about that. But it has nothing to do with this."

"What did they ask for? Money. Not for the so-called rapist to be punished or removed from the classroom or anything rational. Just a half a million dollars. *They* should have
been put in jail."

This line of argument is so off-kilter I don't even know
how to react. "You're scaring me," I hear myself say.

"Remember those people who chained their kid to the ra-
diator, in the eighties? There are sicko Jews, too, Nora. No

one likes to hear it, but it's true." Is she decompensating, falling apart, right now on the phone?

"I'm withdrawing our offer," I say.

For a second or two she is silent, and when she says, "You can't do that," her voice is different, no longer outraged but scared. "That's not how you do business!"

"This isn't business. A girl was raped. Girls, I should say."

"You'll get written up—it's not how this works."

"Are you threatening me?"

"No, no, of course not."

I wait for her to explain how "you'll get written up" was not a threat. I've been at the ED long enough to know that a write-up is the beginning of the end. But when she resumes speaking, she's back in her lawyer voice: "Obviously you're on some mission for justice or something—wasn't that your grandfather's big poem? Anyway, you're trying to settle old scores. I think you should recuse yourself."

"Virtue, not justice. And maybe *you* should."

"There's a lot you don't know, Nora. I'll just say that."

"Like what?"

"We can talk about it when this is behind us."

"If it's related to the case, you'd better tell me now."

"Yeah, well, right now it looks like I have to prepare for a hearing."

She hangs up on me. It's not the first time but I had forgotten how galling it feels and I want to call right back and tell her she's behaving like a teenager. I stare at the phone.

She sounded completely crazy, and I realize I'm frightened—not of being fired, or of physical danger, but of losing her before I've even had a chance to find her. Not the Beth from last night, and certainly not the one from this morning, but the one in the picture from Daisy Kramer's brother's bar mitzvah in 1970—that girl. My first real friend.

33
Nora

I send Jocelyn an email asking if she has a minute—she's going to need to find someone to go to this hearing and argue with Beth because even if I wanted to do that, I wouldn't stand a chance. Time is tight, so after waiting for a reply, I go over to her office, which is empty.

I don't mean that she's just not sitting in it, I mean most of her not-insignificant personal clutter is gone: the napkins, the framed photos. Two plastic wastebaskets are in front of the desk, crammed full of paper and folders. The bust of Elvis remains, holding open the door, but I never believed that was really hers in the first place.

"Weird, right?" says Ktanya, who sits with her back to Jocelyn's door and sees me hovering.

"Yeah," I say. "What happened?"

"No idea. About an hour ago, she came back from somewhere and slammed around for ten minutes and then she left. I heard her rustling around and stuff but I didn't even realize she was *gone* gone till I turned around and looked."

"Check *New York One*," says Joe, a disembodied voice from the next cubicle. Ktanya turns back to her computer and opens the news website.

"I don't see anything," she says after a moment of scanning and scrolling.

"All the way at the bottom, on the right," says Joe. "'Education Dept. Officials Skim Funds.'"

"No way," I say, aware that everyone within earshot is now following along. It's weird how suddenly and silently we have united around this nugget of improbable gossip. "I can imagine a lot of things about Jocelyn, but stealing isn't one of them."

"Word," says a voice down the row, maybe Khan.

"It doesn't say anything about Jocelyn," says Ktanya.

"Ray Landi?" says Joe. "That's her boyfriend."

"Oh, come on," says Ktanya. "She's a lesbian. Everyone knows that."

Jocelyn the lesbian seems as unlikely to me as Jocelyn the thief. But I guess a single, childless woman over forty is an anomaly that people feel must be explained. I'd done it myself, to be honest—supplied her with an early avocation to the church, or a ravaging cancer, or a first marriage better left unmentioned . . .

"I need someone to assign an attorney," I announce. No one volunteers. Why would they?

I return to my desk, sit down, and stare passively at the computer. After a minute—or five—the Facebook message window pops up. Beth Winslow, it says. Who?

Nora, are you there?

I stare at the blinking box. I put my fingers on the keyboard and start to type *Yes* but then I back up. Winslow was her son's name, I remember. Beth comments:

Nora is typing it says. So?

Finally, I type what I mean:

—*All too weird.*

—Let's talk. I mean, as friends.

—I'm still on the case, aren't you?

—Getting an adjournment.

This means it goes back into the queue, that someone else will catch it when a new hearing date is scheduled—meanwhile, her guy's payroll is still suspended and he's clocking seven hours a day in the rubber room.

It makes the most sense, she writes. *For both of us.*

—Why?

I wait, but no text appears. Finally, I write: *It makes sense for both of who?*

You and me, obviously, she comes back.

OK, I type, and then click the X to make the window go away. I swivel away from the screen and look at my desk. What just happened? I had all the power and then I didn't. What the fuck?

The piles of manila folders representing my eighty-five other open cases are still sitting there, untouched since yesterday morning, ready to bury me in their tedium. The news of Jocelyn's disappearance has no doubt crackled through the whole office by now and I'm sure some of my coworkers have already given up any pretense of doing their jobs and are openly reading the gossip blogs, reviewing March Madness brackets, texting away on their cell phones . . .

I go back to Facebook and do what I was planning to do twenty minutes ago: look for old Beth. It doesn't take me long to find those bar mitzvah pictures, square-format shots with the blues faded and signs of brittleness at the edges. The first one I stop at shows three girls seated at a round table littered with plates of cake and cans of Tab. Behind them, unlit but unmistakable because of the mirror-embroidered hippie dress that was almost identical to the one I had, is Beth—as much of a flower child as any twelve-year-old could have wanted to be, her dark bangs grazing her eyelashes, her dangly earrings glittering. I was so angry at her for getting that dress, for copying me. The next picture is of Daisy's parents visiting a table with various Academy teachers and also members of the kitchen and maintenance staff—the Kramers were good liberals. Bob Rasmussen is there, too, as broad-shouldered and rabbity-faced as I remembered. And he is wearing a dashiki. What a fuckwad. I click forward, searching for the image that has stuck in my memory and, two shots later, there it is: the dance floor, with Beth well in frame, doing the shoulder-shivery Frug move that used to make me embarrassed for her.

The first time I saw this image online, it took me straight back to 1970. Beth was the first person I knew to begin converting her schoolgirl hair into a proper mane by bending forward from the waist and tossing it into high-volume disarray. It struck me then as a hideous affectation—so very *not* the act of "a natural woman." Now, I realize that she had a vision of herself as a sexual being, even then, and that intimidated me. Like Rasmussen, she had complete certainty of her own allure and I hated both of them for it. My eye drifts to the photo's caption and I notice that Beth has been tagged since I last was here: "Beth Winslow," it says, in the blue color that means the link is clickable. I wonder why she thinks she needs a pseudonym. Of course, I click.

Her profile picture looks like it was taken outdoors by someone who loves her. It's beautiful: her smile is an unselfconscious blaze of gums and teeth and has the sense of self that only comes from time. I wonder if I have ever looked that way—I must have but I've never really had a boyfriend who liked taking my picture. Maybe I've never much liked having my picture taken. I mean not the way Beth evidently does, and always has. Exploring her albums, I see what I always see on Facebook: beach vacation; fancy dinner of some kind; hiking, swathed in Gore-Tex; clowning around at the Piazza San Marco. I don't see any kids, though, and the husband is apparently camera shy—he's in the pictures as an arm, a shoulder, a partial face. There is only one of him and her together full-length, standing in front of a fireplace in what I take to be a nice restaurant or a fancy hotel—they are dressed up. He is tall, bald, and colorless, older than she is—a perfect dentist or insurance agent with his pretty wife in a black cocktail dress and sparkly necklace. The life she always wanted. Have I not met her at every dinner party or friend's kid's bar mitzvah/graduation/wedding I've ever attended? How many of the other well-meaning lefty suburbanites I've known lead double lives as hookers, or pervert-defenders? The imaginary Beth I've been traveling with all these years was a pliable figure, a mental Barbie, but the new Beth is chimeric, confounding.

I page back through her recent pictures. Now I see that what she is actually doing in the Piazza San Marco is the "exit, stage left" pose: one elbow cocked backward, the other hand leading out, both shoulders slightly raised. It was the tagline of a cartoon character from our childhood, a giant pink cat who lisped—Snagglepuss, a favorite of Rasmussen's. I'm sure *that* was some poor girl's nickname, eventually. It's amazing that I can recognize this gesture, that it has survived all these years. I page back to the two of them, standing up in formal clothes; I look at his size and his shape instead of his face and coloring. He is a full foot taller than she is, which would make him six foot four, and he squares his shoulders in a suit coat the same way he did in a dashiki.

It's Rasmussen. Has he had her all along?

34

Nora

On the blackboard, the stethoscope shape of the ovaries, uterus, and vagina is centered between a needlessly buxom pair of inverted parentheses representing a woman's torso. Rasmussen is describing the relationship between the menstrual cycle and fertility from the point of view of when it's okay or not okay to fuck. He doesn't say "fuck," he says "have sex," of course. He is certainly the most reasonable-sounding person I have ever heard utter the word "vagina." He is not trying to make trouble when he tells us, "You can actually tell when this happens, although the first few times you probably won't know what it is," but the whole situation is so unbearable to me that I can't help but argue.

"That's impossible!" I call out, while he has his back to us. "We don't have skin inside us so we don't have nerves. Anyway, obviously we can't feel a practically microscopic cell detaching. That would be like feeling an eyelash fall off."

But as soon as he turns away from the blackboard, I see the self-satisfied smirk on his face and I know I have only made things worse.

"You say you can't feel pain in your organs, Nora?"

"I said it would be scientifically impossible to feel an ovum doing anything."

"Any one of you young ladies have personal experience here?" Bob asks the room. My classmates practically leap out of their seats with offense and righteous indignation ("Like we'd tell you!" "Out of bounds!" "Gross!") but he loves nothing more than a fight.

"I think 'he who smelt it dealt it' would be the operative principle here, Tiddlywinks," he says, shooting a look at the screechiest screecher, who blushes ferociously. Then he sweeps the rest of us with his smug I've-got-you-exactly-where-I-want-you look. "In any case, I'm certain that most of you have first-hand experience with which you can enlighten Nora." He returns to the board and starts drawing chromosomes.

Relief. He's not going to make an example of me.

"Don't worry, Nora, you'll have a body worth looking at someday," he adds. My classmates laugh at me. I want to fly across the room and stab him in the throat with my Flair pen.

"Anyway, I'll keep my back turned and on the count of three, I want any of you who've felt something like, I don't know, pain? during your period to raise your hand so Nora can see."

The hands shoot up. Turns out it's everyone in the damn room but me and Daisy. "Okay," starts Bob. The hands shoot back down. He turns around and takes a step toward my desk, smirking for all he's worth. "'Nuff said?" My stabbing fantasy resumes but it's also ridiculous and I see that. I would be like a gnat on his giant carcass. And anyway the rest of them are all apparently women now, and I am some kind of null set, a firework that didn't explode. And the worst part is there was something going on in my body from pretty much the instant he announced the topic of today's lesson. His unsexy description of the mechanics, which assumed we would all soon be using this knowledge if we weren't already, had set off all kinds of—not fantasies, not ideas—just seeds of thoughts, starting to feel watered and warmed, and that was probably why I had to yell out my objection in the first place. I had to stop the shoots. And now that feeling and the misery of having been wrong, the shame of being flat and sexless, and the rage that I know better than to express are all mixed up in my gut. I will never forgive him for this. I have been drawing in my notebook—angry squares inside of squares inside of squares made with lines so dark I have flattened the tip of my pen. When I finally look up again, everyone is fully absorbed in the lesson about dominant and recessive traits.

35
Nora

I walk home from work, head into the wind, trying not to think about Beth and Bob together but it's like trying not to think of an elephant. She married him. She sleeps in his bed. He didn't die, or go to jail, or fall into a hole in the earth. And what's more, he is loved. The ways Beth tried to manipulate me into settling the case this afternoon now seem diabolical instead of pathetic. She's not just accidentally defending a bent teacher, she's an accomplice. Singer and Rasmussen and how many others? Was her story about being a hooker even true? The one about losing her son?

I think again about that eerie phone call last night. The memory of her sobbing now has a different cast: just by being his willing partner, referring to him casually as "my husband," she has behaved monstrously and she knows it. Him, I can't even think about. Not really.

How can it be that I wind up alone, and *they* get domesticity? This thought feels like it will bury me if I let it. I have to talk to someone else about this or I will go out of my mind. But the obvious person to talk to about it is Beth herself. Who else?

My mother. But I don't have one of those, either. And when I did, I hated her. Is this self-pity? I think of Mom's last day— she was comatose but had a beautiful East River view seen only by myself and the nurses. The sight of her stricken figure, curled like a comma in that mechanical bed, filled my lungs, drowning me. All the things I'd never get to say, all the things I'd failed to explain, all the missed and broken connections that bound us to each other . . . It was too much for one person to mourn.

Inside the apartment, I head straight to the master bathroom, start the multi-headed shower, and leave my clothes in a pile on the floor. Under the main showerhead, with all three horizontal jets pelting my torso, I focus on erasure—scrubbing with my coarse plastic sponge, getting behind my ears and between my toes, telling myself that I can scrape away all the residue if I put in enough effort. Because, what else? What now?

In my bathrobe, I lie down on the library floor and look up at my grandfather's mural. The constellation I see first is Cassiopeia and from her I can infer Perseus, Andromeda, and Ursa Minor. As a child I knew more of what those names represented but none of it has stayed with me, nor do I know how the shapes I see—the W, the square, and the saucepan—add up to a queen, a soldier, or the smaller of two bears. I grasp at the idea of order, of stories embedded in random patterns, of pictures that go on looking the same to the people standing on Earth despite eons of distance and oceans of time. I used to think if I lay here long enough thinking these thoughts I could go there: to mythological time, to deep space. I used to think there was a different world possible for me, and that getting there was just a matter of blurring my eyes in a certain way, or of saying certain words in Latin or Greek, or of taking one good picture. That was what I used to think.

36
Nora

While I'm lying on the library floor, my cell phone rings. The display says "NYC Ed Dept," which I think must mean Jocelyn. She's the only person at work who has my cell number. I'm kind of afraid to answer it, but also grateful for an opportunity to get out of my own head.

"Where *are* you?" says the woman's voice on the other end. Not Jocelyn's but it's a noisy background and I don't know who it is. "I think you have the wrong number," I start to say, but the caller interrupts me:

"Nora! Get over here! We're at Morton's!"

Morton's is next door to the office. "I don't understand," I say, although now I recognize that my caller is Gina.

"We're at the bar. We're celebrating..." She says something I don't understand.

"What?"

"Jocelyn's lottery win. She and Myra's cousins won the Powerball! Ninety-three million!"

"Who's Myra?"

"You know Myra, who cleans the bathroom? Isn't that awesome? Anyway, I'll let her tell it. One sec."

As I hear the phone thrust into the cacophony at the bar, I rewind my vision of Jocelyn-the-embezzler and restore the eccentric-nut-from-Catholic-school version of her I had previously been maintaining. I can hear Gina saying, "Joss! Talk to Nora!" but she is drowned out by a group of voices counting down from ten, which I conclude has to do with drinking shots. I hear Gina shrieking with laughter. The phone is forgotten and I hang up.

I'm standing in front of my closet, unable to decide whether to put on clothes or pajamas when the phone rings again. Again, it's the NYC Ed Dept.

"Seriously, get over here," says Gina. "It's Friday night. You're never going to see this woman again. Don't you want to wish her well?"

It's impossible to say no to Gina.

Despite the fact that it's fifty paces from my office, ten minutes from my house, and offers six-dollar wine at happy hour, I've never been inside Morton's. The double doors of the restaurant open into a plush reception area where not checking my coat feels like an act of aggression. I tell the seventeen-year-old hostess, "I'm going to the bar," by way of an apology, but she seems oblivious and in I go. The place is packed with men in suits. I guess they are the lawyers and judges who work in the courts, because they are not the stockbrokers and media moguls of Brooklyn Heights. I elbow my way through the initial scrum. Then I see them, occupying a large high table arrayed with barstools—a surprising assortment of my coworkers that includes Ktanya, Joe, Myra, Gina, Jocelyn, Jessica, and three or four others I recognize but haven't spoken to since being introduced on my first day. Edward, a silent, skinny guy with long hair, claps me on the shoulder and says, "Hey, what are you drinking?" I point at his beer glass and say thanks as Gina notices me and starts waving me over to where she and Jocelyn are sharing a stool. Jocelyn is almost unrecognizable: her hair's in a ponytail and she's wearing a red leather motorcycle jacket. Moreover, she looks dazed. When I get to her side, I say "Congratulations! I'm so happy for you!" and find that it's true, I am.

She says, "I'm going to learn to surf!"

"That's great," I say. "It's perfect!"

"I grew up practically at Breezy Point, but my father wouldn't let me. He said it was unladylike and a waste of time."

I nod.

"So fuck him!" says Jocelyn, rather loudly and slams the rest of her drink. Various others echo her sentiment and knock back their drinks—including Myra, who says something I suppose to be the equivalent in Spanish. I wonder how many cousins she has. I'm sure I learned how to say "cousin" somewhere in my six years of Spanish but all I can come up with is "novio," which I'm pretty sure means fiancé so I just smile at her and say "Congratulations!" She is still wearing her khaki shirt and chinos with the cleaning contractor's company name over the breast pocket. At this point, Edward hands me my beer and Gina mimes a toast at me so I drink.

"What's your 'fuck 'em,' Nora?" Gina yells across the table.

I don't have a ready answer to this question—or maybe I have too many. "Fuck history," I say finally, but this happens at a momentary gap in the background noise and my comment seems to hang there, gathering social unease like flies on a dead thing.

"Fuck history!" says Gina, raising her glass as though this is a perfectly normal toast, and then mouths *Awk-ward!* at me. I shrug. She shrugs back.

"Fuck that fucker most of all," Jocelyn adds in a drunken slur, and we all drink again.

37
Nora

Speaking of history, this is my grandfather's famous poem, "The Pursuit of Virtue at Brooklyn Heights." It's about the abolitionist preacher Henry Ward Beecher, whose adulterous affair with a parishioner was a nationwide scandal in 1874.

> Wandering, I found my way
> Like any man of letters,
> Across the bridge, to Brooklyn's quay—
> A free man, closely fettered.
> I came to see the place where once,
> A great man fell to circumstance.
>
> "I can't abide his infamy."
> So testified a neighbor.
> On Orange Street, at Plymouth Church
> The man of virtue wavered.
> He told the word of God on high.
> He lived the word of God—a lie.
>
> Pilgrim preacher, hypocrite.
> I see him cast in bronze,
> Freer of slaves! Transcendent wit!

Yet, man of flesh and bone.
What say you, sage? What will become
Of men like thee? of anyone?

And though I hear not human speech,
His answer rends the air:
"Three Godly things are all I've gleaned:
A hand, a plow, a star!"
And love? I ask him with my eyes,
Love that comes in strange disguise?
What say you then?

"I say that it was ever thus.
The 'Heights' of ours are depths, the same.
Let men rejoice, who are not dust.
As none have ever died of shame."

I, too, live at Brooklyn Heights,
I planted—and a garden grew.
Of fruits or weeds, I know not yet,
Nor will I know. Nor ever knew.

My daughter wakes, a child of ten,
Her nightgown, mothlike in its sheen.
She watches me in innocence.
She watches me as in a dream.

38
Nora

I wake up on Saturday feeling lonely. I have never used that word to describe my own feelings before. *Solitary* maybe, or *moody* or *introspective*, but those were all ways of mitigating the underlying need and now I just feel the thing itself, as plain as hunger or thirst. I've always told myself this is what drives people to behave stupidly: to marry badly, to get pregnant when they can't afford to have kids, to befriend people who wind up stealing from them, or who just suck them dry with their neediness—all the entanglements I have so successfully avoided.

At fourteen, I thought Beth's life was better than mine because it looked more normal: married parents, "interior decorating," a place to go in the summer, new clothes in the fall. And, despite her sexual adventures and her "losing my mind" letter, I had always assumed that as an adult she would revert to type, that she was living in suburbia, having babies, doing all the things I would never do. That way, I could look at my own prickliness and solitude as choices, proof of my integrity and deep convictions. *At least I'm not like Beth* is a sentence I've been saying to myself all this time. I still want to say it, but the meaning is upside down now. Have I been the one doing things right?

It isn't that hard to track her down. There are hundreds of Elizabeth Cohens in Brooklyn, but only three Beth Winslows: one in the Heights, which I'm sure she would have mentioned; one in Williamsburg; and one on Eastern Parkway. The one in Williamsburg turns out to be in the Hasidic part and the one on Eastern Parkway is right across from the museum in a building a lot like this one: prewar, a dozen or so stories, green awning, brown doorman. I decide that I will go to the farmer's market and then call her, saying I am in the neighborhood. If her husband is still out of town, I will go see her, and if he's there, I won't. I'm not scared of him—he's an old man now anyway. But I don't want to see him. What I want is her explanation.

At Borough Hall, the 2 train comes right away and is nearly empty. There's something almost pleasant about sitting in the middle of the long, gray bench with nothing across from me but my own reflection. Near the doors sits a black man with his young daughter, clearly kicking off child custody Saturday. The little girl has yellow tights on and is reading Harry Potter. Her dad is staring into his phone like it's some kind of oracle.

I get off at Grand Army Plaza and walk the semicircular maze to the park entrance in a stiff, cold wind. The park is always further from the subway than I remember and I still haven't figured out the best way to navigate these intersections. It starts to sleet. I put up the hood of my coat. I pull out my phone and call Beth, turning away from the wind, or trying to. Then I realize I don't have her number in my contacts. I also don't have the internet—my phone isn't smart and my down coat isn't waterproof. I am getting pelted. The only thing I can think to do is head for her presumed building. At least I can take shelter in the lobby—I assume it will have couches, or something, but of course I am stopped there by the doorman, nicely. I say, "Beth Winslow?" and as he rings her he tells me, "10F," and gestures toward the elevators, because of course I couldn't look more harmless and I knew the codename. But on my way up in the elevator, I panic. I press the button for 6, but I've passed it, then for 8 but too late, and the car stops, the door opens on 10. I hold the Door Open button, hesitating: she will be expecting me, but what if he's there?

Well, what if he is?

Beth is standing in her open doorway when I get there. She looks like she got dressed in a hurry—barefoot, jeans and a sweater, no makeup. "Not that I'm not glad to see you," she says, "but you could have called."

"I was at the farmer's market and it started sleeting," I say.

"How'd you get my address?"

"Used my skills," I say, embarrassed by the relentlessness of my pursuit. "I really wanted to talk to you. We left things so unsettled."

"Come in," she says, and holds open the door. There are no lights on in the apartment and though there's a wall of windows across the room, the place seems gloomy and lifeless.

"Is your husband home?" I ask.

"No," she says. "Sit down. Do you want coffee?"

I nod.

The living room is large and full of stuff: books, a substantial cache of records, magazines, piles of paper. As my eyes adjust I see that in better light it must be a pleasant room—

well-used brown leather couch, rust-colored velvet armchair, rush-seated rocker, Native American rug. It looks a bit like Rasmussen's old living room on Willow Street, but more refined, or maybe just cleaner: the magazines are stacked neatly, as are the piles of paper. Beth comes back in and sits down in the velvet chair, putting down our coffee cups side by side—mine in front of my perch on the couch. She scans the room as though looking for something. "I have some things here that I bet you'd get a kick out of," she says. "From when we were kids."

"Really?" I sound so false, but I haven't actually figured out what I'm here to say.

"There's this clay sculpture of an owl that you made. Do you remember it?"

I shake my head.

"You were a wise old owl back then," she says.

"Wiseass, more like."

She smiles but isn't buying it. I see that she's fidgeting, and that she's not wearing any of her jewelry. Hail ticks against the windows as we sit in awkward silence. Just as she is about to stand up, announcing "Anyway—" I blurt:

"Listen, I figured it out. About you and Bob."

Her head zips around like a falcon's spotting prey, but she stays seated, obviously weighing whether I can possibly mean what she thinks I do. "You what?"

"Pictures on Facebook."

She tilts her head, mentally reviewing her online photos. "How?"

"Exit stage left, for one thing."

She nods and then smiles ruefully. "I mean, not that it's a secret, exactly. The statute of limitations is up. But we just try and keep the past separate from the present as much as we can."

"And use a false name."

"That's something else. I mean, you're right, but Winslow is because of my son." She shifts in her seat, recrosses her legs, thinks. Then she looks at me. "Do you want to see his picture?"

She gets up without waiting for my answer and unshelves a photo album from across the room. I see her hesitate and then grab a second volume before returning to her chair. She leafs through the first binder until she finds what she's looking for, a school portrait of a young teenaged boy with curly hair and braces on his teeth. He's wearing a black T-shirt with something printed on it but I can't tell what. He has her smile. He looks motherless. I don't know why I think that, but I do. I've always read a lot into photographs.

"How recent?" I ask.

"Last year. My ex sends them to my lawyer so he doesn't have to deal with me asking." She fidgets with the other pages of the album, letting them slip from her fingers one by one.

"Are you in touch at all?"

She shakes her head.

"But he must remember . . . ?"

"I think so, too," she says. "But the deal was no contact."

"Does he think you're dead?"

"I don't know what they told him. Maybe."

I close the album and set it aside on the coffee table. I do feel sorry for her, but I am not done with the Rasmussen questions.

"Is it okay if—I want to know more about you and Rasmussen. How long . . . ?"

She shakes her head as though to clear it, then takes her long hair in one hand and starts to twist it. She talks without looking at me.

"We met again in ninety-eight. It was like finding out someone I thought was dead was still alive. I mean, I'd never forgotten him, but I didn't think I'd ever see him again."

"Who found who?"

"Blind date. Well not exactly blind—set up by a friend who knew us both from Whores and Perverts Anonymous . . ."

It takes me a second to realize she means their twelve-step program. "And you were still into him?"

"It wasn't like that. It was more like finding a lost part of myself. Like he connected the dots for me between who I am and who I used to be . . . know what I mean?"

I do. Because it's what I wanted her to do for me, and in some ways, it's what she has done. I don't really want to know the details of her life with Rasmussen, I just want to know I didn't imagine it. I needed to view the body.

"At least now I understand why you were so weird about the case."

"I wasn't weird; I was keeping you guessing. That's my job."

"Which doesn't erase the fact that your husband's a predator."

She winces at my choice of words. "Don't be so simplistic. It doesn't suit you."

"But he is, right?"

"I didn't fix him, no. But I will be divorcing him, if that's any consolation."

She opens the second photo album and flips through a few pages. "Look, I found this the other night—this picture . . ." And she hands the book to me, turning it right side up as she does.

"Look at how beautiful!" she says.

It's an enlarged black-and-white photograph of a young girl, seemingly naked, with her long hair covering her left eye, her left shoulder, and most of her childlike left breast. I have seen it before, and many times since in my mind's eye. It's the picture of Tamsin that has always meant "Rasmussen the Rapist" to me. The blurry background is the Academy darkroom. Examining it closely, I now recognize my own adolescent attempts at documentary photography clipped to the clothesline behind the girl in the foreground: the telephone nook in afternoon light; the cat Anna, her coat ruffled with static electricity; my mother, in her sealskin coat, lipstick gleaming. Why, I wonder, are my pictures there? I've never remembered that before. And so I look again at Tamsin, aka Christmas, the girl in the picture, trapped in a mesh of light and shadow, and wrapped also, partly, in the mask of her own long hair. And I see that she's not Tamsin at all. She's me.

"I never let him do that!" I say, as though the picture itself has just said the words, "He raped you." But flashes of memory have already started up a counterargument—him pulling my shirt over my head, the hot lamplight on my shoulder, how alien and brilliant I felt when he first looked at me through the camera. . . . I look at the child in the photo—she has no idea how vulnerable she is. Now I remember everything—that instant of joy, followed by immediate shame and the impulse to deny and erase. It went no further than the photographs, but afterward I felt that I had lost everything: my strength, my shell. That was why I pushed Beth away then, so she wouldn't find out how weak I was. I'm looking straight at her, wanting her to understand why I was so mean to her almost as much as I want her to disappear completely.

"But *you're* not a victim," she says. "Are you? You don't seem like a victim to me."

Victim? No. But I hear a gasp come out of my chest that sounds almost like retching—a physical reaction I can't control. The tears that come with it seem to be for everything at once: my mother, my cat, my photographer's eye, my shining youth. . . . When Beth tries to put her hand on my arm, I swat it away with all my might.

"I'm sorry, Nora," she says.

"What for?"

"I don't know. Disappointing you?"

"You didn't," I say, between sobs. I shake my head as I try to breathe normally, wiping my eyes with my wrists. "You just lived your life," I say finally. "It didn't turn out the way it was supposed to. No one's does."

After I have had a glass of water and washed my face in the kitchen sink (I have no interest in entering their shared bathroom), she accompanies me downstairs in the elevator. It's still sleeting, but Beth has called a car service and given them my address. She has also wrapped the old photo between two pieces of cardboard and put it into a manila envelope. I want to look at it again. I also want to destroy it. As the elevator door slides open in the lobby, I can see that she expects me to say something to her that will make it okay to part this way, but I can't, and neither can she, so I step into the lobby and she places her finger on the button that makes the door close faster.

The car service smells like coconut air freshener, so I open the window a bit and ride home with my eyes closed and my face occasionally stung by sleet.

39
Bob

Hello, I'm Bob, an addict and a pervert. I can call myself a pervert but I don't really believe I'm a pedophile because that's an old guy who bribes little girls with candy, or a priest who tells the altar boy that God will punish him if he tells, and a pervert is an outlaw, a badass. They write songs about him, right? So if I sit down next to some young thing on the bus, and watch her flick her hair for the idiot across the aisle, and see the curve in her leg that doesn't yet completely resemble a woman's leg, and smell the sweat she isn't yet old enough to recognize as an odor, I am participating in a tradition as American as "Sweet Little Sixteen" and as old as "Darling, Clementine."

Unfortunately, when my memory of the girl and her sweat fades she becomes all the other girls, and the hatred they have for me is stuck inside me like a meal I'll never digest. I can argue my way out of it just like the rest of you but we all know what we did. What we do.

I rescued my first wife from her father when she was just fifteen and the stories she told me about that old bastard made me realize it could be done. Only then, once I'd done it, there was no going back. She put up with it—programmed, right? But I hated myself. So I thought if I had kids of my own I wouldn't have those feelings about other people's. You laugh because you thought the same thing. And it worked for a while, right? I saw how helpless they were and I was their defender. That was a job I knew I could do. There was an ice cream man who stopped near our house in Brooklyn. Sal. A fat fuck. I could have torn that guy in half when he looked at my Doria, in her summer dress with the sailboats on it.

Sometimes I think every guy whose job keeps him near kids is one of us. Basketball coach, pediatrician, the guy who runs the batting cages, the mall cop . . . all torturing themselves, and giving in, and getting caught, but there's no need to get caught. Even if someone forgives you—marries you, even—it's never over. There's no end, which is what we really want, what we're all driving toward. Isn't it? A way out? So here's what else I know. There isn't one. You think: I could just shoot myself. But what you don't think is, what if I don't die?

I went to see my son this morning—a place some of you might know, the state hospital. They may call it a hospital but it smells like a prison. He's there because he can't take care of himself and hasn't been able to since he was eighteen. He got into a good school, smart kid, then shot himself in the head. No tuition refund, by the way. Doesn't matter. No one can afford to pay what it costs to keep someone alive who doesn't want life.

Archer didn't recognize me; I'm an old guy now and in his head it's still 1978. Of course he looks a lot like me, now, but I guess he's not looking in the mirror much. His hair's still red, what there is of it. And he has his mother's black eyes. But his mother always looked right at me, even when she hated my guts, and my son doesn't know how to do that. He looks at the ceiling, the corner up there, to his left. And sometimes he shakes his head no, and sometimes yes, and then back to no and he'll keep at it until the giant black dude who's guarding him makes him stop. The fact that he's guarded by a giant tells me that he's capable of serious damage to person and property but all I saw was the head-shaking thing. He's not a vegetable. He says things. He says, *I shouldn't of done it,* which I think means shot himself. And he says, *They put me in jail for doing dirty things to girls*, which isn't true. He bites his nails like I do. I told him he didn't do anything wrong. I told him his father was the one who should be in jail. And then he told me that he'd shot that guy, too. Blew his head right off. *I shouldn't of done it*, he said.

40
Naomi

My son looked right into my eyes when he shot me. My thought was, *He has me dead to rights*. His father wasn't even there—he'd not spoken to Bob in months. Not since that spring when Tamsin showed up in Rutland and Archer realized for the first time what had been going on back at our house in Brooklyn—why he'd lost the happy life he'd so resented being taken from. He'd missed the corner candy store with the comic books, and the basketball game in the schoolyard at P.S. 8. He missed being in with the black dudes in a way other white kids weren't. Vermont had nothing he wanted, he said. And then, one day, Christmas shows up and starts talking to him like a grownup, because he looked like one at seventeen, and the next thing you know he's locked in his room all summer writing in notebooks and listening to music that sounds like screams and machines. We shouldn't have let him go off to school that fall, but we did. I saw him last in his cinderblock dorm room. It was an empty, empty place.

But he didn't shoot his father, he shot me and then he shot himself—it's best he remembers it the other way, though. If memory's even what's happening in my son's brain, poor soul.

I notice Bob can't hardly say my name. That Archer would shoot me like that—would kill his mama that *he* loved most in the world—that's the part his father's got no words for: that the harm just goes on, like a stone in the quarry sending out ripples. I'd told Bob all about it from the get-go, but he knew it already, too. It's an old refrain—Bob's Swedish folk might've had the words a bit different than my Scots-Cherokee, but in the end we sing it all together, like a hymn. No one thinks that the worst will happen to them.

41
Nora

It's not quite three o'clock when I get back to my apartment. I put the envelope with the photo in it up high on my shelf in the library and then I go directly to bed, waking at dusk to the clang of the downstairs buzzer. I realize it's been ringing for a while. I make my way up the hall and lift the intercom receiver. My voice is raspy when I say, "Hello?"

"We have your cat, Miss Nora. Victor is coming up with him now."

I think I may be dreaming.

"He was outside by the laundry. Eliza heard him." Eliza is the super's daughter. She's eight.

I put down the receiver, cross the kitchen, and open the outer elevator door, staring at the inner one as though I could pull the car upward and open it by telekinesis. I have not waited for anything or anyone with a heart so full since I can remember.

When the elevator arrives, the cat saunters out and right past me, heading for food.

"There he is!" says Victor, still in the elevator car, proud of his power to reunite us. His little girl is standing next to him, in her nightgown, smiling with profound delight. He has his hand on her shoulder and he looks as proud of her as she is of herself.

"Thank you!" I say. "Thank you, Eliza!" I want to hug her almost as much as I want to reclaim Tin Man. But the elevator door is closing and I follow the cat, instead, falling to my knees to grab him under the forelegs. I want to hug him forever but he slips away, bleating and hovering in the corner where his dish sits, empty.

I watch him consume an entire can of Paul Newman's daughter's cat food. I barely look away while he then cleans himself from stem to stern, yanking vigorously with his teeth on each hind toenail. I love him with my eyes for as long as that takes.

Done cleaning, Tin Man saunters into the long hallway and heads straight for my bedroom, tail high, like a clockwork cat. I hear him land on my down comforter with a *whomf* and I follow him there. I push my nose into his belly fur—a maneuver he barely tolerates most times but he is now too bone-tired to resist. I breathe in the warm, powdery scent of his soft undercoat and it reminds me of the trace remnants of my mother's perfume: how her sealskin coat smelled when it returned to the hall closet after a night at the theater or the opera; how she herself smelled when I buried my face in her neck and kissed her goodnight; and even how her clothes smelled when I retrieved them from the hospital and there was no more life in them at all.

I should sleep the sleep of the dead—the cat does—and at first I do too, but then I wake up again and it feels like morning but it isn't. I'm not having nightmares; what wakes me is the feeling of having an appointment, of needing to be somewhere. It's so keen that I eventually get out of bed to retrieve my laptop. There is nothing on my calendar. Maybe it's some-one's birthday—someone I no longer celebrate? I run down the list of dead people and ex-boyfriends but it's not that, either. Walking down the hall toward the kitchen, I find myself stopping at the doorway to the library. And then I know what the appointment is that I think I have.

I retrieve the manila envelope from the shelf and take it with me to the kitchen. I pour a splash of scotch into a glass of milk and sit down at the breakfast nook. I slide the picture out so it's sitting in front of me on the table, like a small meal, and I look.

I look more closely at the girl this time: half-naked, half-showing herself to the camera. I look at the flare of light on her left shoulder and the murky shapes in the room behind her. I look at her shiny, abundant hair and her childish torso, through which her ribs show faintly. She has pronounced collarbones, as I still do. Her skin has not yet met acne, or even chicken pox (that came later that same year). Her ears are not yet pierced, her legs have never been shaved, she doesn't own a brassiere. But I look at her face and it is my face. Not an early draft, but me just as I am this very moment: half-defiant, half-hidden, determined to observe and know, but not asking any questions I don't really want to hear answered, either. I didn't want him to fuck me, but I *had* wanted him to see me and exclaim my beauty—wanted it so badly I took off my clothes.

But instead of feeling jubilant afterward, I had only felt defiled. I'd said no to his gropings, but then I'd given in to his smarmy power, after all. He turned off the lamp and put his camera away, and suddenly all I could think about was how

I might erase this horrible mistake. That I had to cancel my participation in the summer trip was obvious. And I also had to extricate myself from my friendship with Beth—she would see through me, otherwise. I told her that we just took pictures, that nothing happened. But something did happen. As Tamsin said, we can't unhappen it.

I take the photo back to the bedroom and lean it against the wall on top of my dresser, where I can see it from my bed. Let's see what it feels like to live with her, I think. It can't be any worse than trying to make her disappear. I lie down beside Tin Man in his cat coma, and hug my pillow. It's not over, but the part where I meet my shadow at the crossroads is behind me, at least.

Monday
February 23, 2009

42
Nora

On Monday morning, I have three messages on my work phone—all from the same 345 number, someone's cell phone. It's unlikely to be any of my usual counterparts. The attorneys who make their livings suing the ED don't generally work on weekends. Of course, it could be Beth. For all I know she was bluffing about the adjournment and the Singer hearing is still on at eleven. So I call the hearing office, and wait on hold, and find out that that is exactly what she has done.

I rap on the partition that separates me from Ktanya. I stand on tiptoe so I can see her through the window in our cubicle wall. "That case from last week is on in an hour. What should I do?"

"Get yourself over to Livingston Street."

"And do what?"

"Represent. Read your notes into the record. At least you'll have shown up. Chances are your opposing won't, and then it's their forfeit."

"What if she does?" I ask, meaning "show up" but my phone rings again and it's the 345 number, so I answer it.

The hearing room is windowless, dingy, and about the size of the dining room in my grandfather's apartment. Seated at the far end of a brown, fold-up banquet table is a stenographer, with her machine open in front of her, as well as a bag of Cheez Doodles. She's wearing a tracksuit. I sit down on one of the rolling office chairs at the near end of the table but it's missing a wheel, so I switch over to the next one, which has a disconcerting stain on the seat. I smile anxiously at the stenographer, who says, "You're new."

I nod and introduce myself. Her name is Lana something-or-other. I knew, of course, that these hearings were not the same as legal proceedings, that they don't follow the rules of evidence or procedure the way a real court does, but I was not prepared for this slackness—the thing is supposed to start in less than five minutes and me and Lana are the only ones here. Then the door opens and a mousy-looking woman peeks in, and then shuts the door without entering. "Wrong room, I guess," I say. Lana says, "No one likes to be the first to show up. It shows weakness or something."

I unpack my bag; I figure that at a bare minimum I can read aloud from a great deal of paper. At eleven exactly, a young woman enters—Zadie Collins, owner of the 345 number: a former student of Singer's. We barely had time to discuss what she might say, and I regret that I did not coach her on what to wear, because she has on leggings in lieu of pants and also a largely transparent yellow shirt underneath which a red bra is evident. She shakes my hand, sits down in the broken chair next to mine, and spends the next three minutes alternately forming her long hair into a sloppy topknot and poking the keys of her cell phone.

The hearing officer arrives at five after. She is my age, African American, and has an impressive blonde weave as well as a substantial gold crucifix. She nods at Lana and raises an eyebrow at me, ignoring Zadie. "Let's get started," she says, at which point Beth enters the room, alone. She nods professionally at the hearing officer, then at the rest of us. When that's over she trains her gaze on Zadie's face, smiling a weird mixture of appraisal and approval. The hearing officer formally introduces herself—Katrina Adams—then states the time, the hearing number and Harold Singer's name. Then she says, "With me are . . ." and the rest of us introduce ourselves. I say my name is Eleanor, and this makes me realize that I am really doing this thing, representing the Education Department and, more specifically, the girl-victims of this teacher who really isn't Bob Rasmussen, this enemy I've never even met.

Officer Adams refers to him as "the employee" as she reads the individual charges that are meant to add up to his dismissal: accompanied a female ninth-grade student to the lunchroom at such time when neither had cause to be at said place, made unnecessary notations constituting sexual innuendo on the homework of several students, referred to the sexual orientation of another teacher as "equally bent" when confronted by a student about his own behavior, and so on.

"But wait, doesn't *he* have to be here?" I ask. For I have promised Zadie and friends an opportunity to confront their former teacher.

"I'm afraid not," says Officer Adams.

Beth smiles to herself, shaking her head over my naïveté. I do not recognize the sad old friend I met on Saturday, nor the desperate-seeming woman who showed up on the phone last week. We are back to being cutthroat opponents. She will not meet my gaze.

On my left, Zadie is still monitoring her phone, which she is holding under the edge of the conference table as though this is fooling anyone. She notices me noticing and shows me the screen, which says, "G train fucked," and she makes a kind of facial shrug. I mouth *Put it away* and feel like an old fart. But what else do we need to know? The classmates she said she would round up are stuck in Williamsburg. So much for Gina's "backup singers" strategy.

"Does the Department have anything to add?" asks Officer Adams. "That's you," she adds, after I have looked at her blankly for a moment. And then she says, "I see you have a witness."

"Witnesses," says Zadie.

"I wasn't notified of this," says Beth, calmly.

"We only made contact this morning," I say.

"We're former students of his," says Zadie.

"Objection," says Beth, as the hearing room door opens and two more young people walk in, a young man and woman. The woman looks around, checking our faces nervously; the man just looks at Beth and smiles a smile of what truly looks like joy.

"Please take a seat, we're in session," says Officer Adams. "And identify yourselves. You first," she says to Zadie. The two girls give their names. The new one, Meredith, has a large tattoo underneath her clavicle that says "strength" in fancy script. The boy announces himself as Ello Cascarelli. "I use ze, zir, zirself," he says.

"What, now?" says Officer Adams.

"Those are my pronouns. Instead of he you say 'ze,' instead of his you say 'zir'—"

"We'll do our best," says Officer Adams, clearly impatient.

I stare at Ello, last seen on Facebook as a pretty girl, presumed dead. The charges against Singer from 2002 weren't upheld because she, the victim, didn't even show up. Now, as Ello, ze is wearing a jacket and tie, and quite fiercely alive.

"Harold Singer was my rapist, on numerous occasions in 2001 and 2002, when I was his student at the Hilda Conkling School," Ello continues, unasked.

"This is not the matter at hand," says Beth, irritated.

"Agreed," says Officer Adams.

"He persuaded me that he could cure my gender dysphoria by arousing me sexually," ze says. "I have a number of handwritten notes from him that will substantiate this claim."

"This matter was previously decided," says Beth.

The hearing officer is obviously frustrated by this complete departure from procedure, but I can see that she is also interested—perhaps out of prurience, but I suspect also a sense of justice. Who hasn't dreamt of coming back to face an oppressor with the tables somehow turned?

"I would ask that the Department's witnesses be sworn in appropriately so that I may consider their testimony," she says. "That means you, young . . . person. And you need to pipe down until you're called on."

Beth is shielding her eyes with one hand and scribbling furiously on her yellow pad, but I can tell that she's not actually writing anything. I know what she looks like when she's faking. And this, more than anything that comes after, tells me that she has nothing to match this, no more tricks up her sleeve. She was assuming I wouldn't get here, wouldn't put on a case, wouldn't matter, in the end, but it seems I do.

After the hearing, I shake hands with Ello, Meredith, and Zadie in the freezing morning air on Livingston Street. Beth has disappeared. "Thank you so much," I say. "That was so brave."

"I just wish I'd been able to do it the first time around," says Ello.

"It must be easier as a man," I say.

"I'm not a man," says Ello. "I'm genderqueer."

And, I guess because I am so flustered, I then say, "I thought you were dead." Ze looks horrified, appropriately. "From your friends' Facebook posts . . ." I try to explain.

Ello laughs a splendid laugh, linking arms with the others. "My friends are such drama queens," ze says. "It was all about them, right?"

"Hey," says Zadie, "we were fifteen!"

The wind is so cold my nose is already numb, but they are so adorable and full of life that I ask them to hold on a second while I take their picture. My phone may not be smart, but it does contain a camera and I know that their feeling of triumph is one I want to capture for myself.

Acknowledgments

Although the Academy is entirely an invention, the *Tis Bottle* looks a lot like the *Turtle*, a volume authored by my own seventh-grade classmates at the now-defunct Woodward School. I am grateful to Sophia Hollander and the brave women she interviewed about their experiences at Woodward for her 2014 *Wall Street Journal* article "Years of Abuse at Brooklyn School Alleged."

I came up with the idea of Nora's grandfather, the rockstar poet, after reading about Edwin Markham, whose "The Man with the Hoe" was—according to the *New York Times*—"the most profitable poem ever written" at the time of his death. I used the poem "He Who Loved Beauty" by Alec Brock Stevenson as a starting point for "The Pursuit of Virtue at Brooklyn Heights."

Brooklyn Heights is where I grew up and now live, but so much has changed. *The Invention of Brownstone Brooklyn* by Suleiman Osman was a helpful (and fascinating) look at the period I was trying to describe.

I wrote an early draft of this book at Yaddo in the summer of 2011, and though not a sentence survives, I am forever grateful for that experience.

Since it took me the better part of ten years to write this novel, the number of friends pressed into service to read, reread, encourage, and commiserate is unbearably long. I am indebted to all, but a few deserve special credit: Julie Applebaum, Joe Gioia, Kara Lindstrom, Naomi Rand, Jenny Snider. Thank you, my dear friends!

Many thanks also to Ann Rittenberg for her interest, effort, and encouragement, and to all at Red Hen Press, for making this book a reality at last.

Biographical Note

Rachel Cline, author of the novels *What to Keep* and *My Liar*, has written for the *New York Times*, *New York*, *More*, *SELF*, and *Tin House*, and is a produced screen and television writer. For five years, she was a screenwriting instructor at the University of Southern California and has taught fiction writing at New York University, Eugene Lang College, and Sarah Lawrence College. She has been a resident at Yaddo, a fellow at Sewanee, and a Girls Write Now mentor. She lives in Brooklyn Heights, a few blocks from where she grew up.